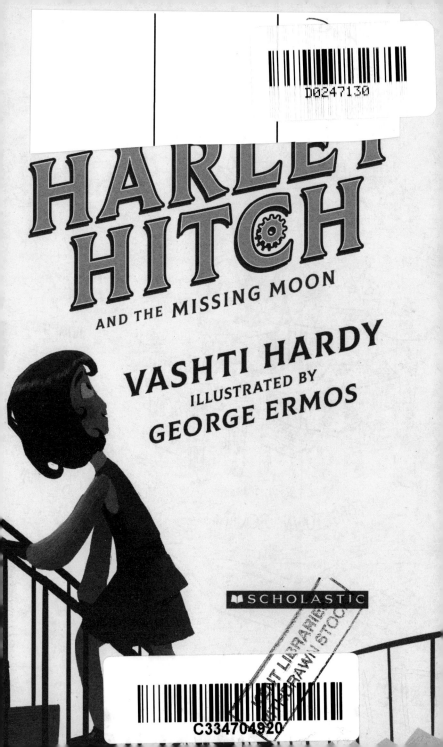

HARLEY HITCH

AND THE MISSING MOON

VASHTI HARDY

ILLUSTRATED BY
GEORGE ERMOS

■ SCHOLASTIC

JUNKYARD of FORGOTTEN MACHINE DREAMS

THE IRON FOREST

OLD MILL

RUSTY RIVER

STAR CHATTER OBSERVATORY

COPPER MOUNTAINS

For Paula

Published in the UK by Scholastic, 2022
Euston House, 24 Eversholt Street, London, NW1 1DB, UK
Scholastic Ireland, 89E Lagan Road, Dublin Industrial Estate,
Glasnevin, Dublin, D11 HP5F

SCHOLASTIC and associated logos are trademarks and/or
registered trademarks of Scholastic Inc.

Text © Vashti Hardy, 2022
Illustrations © George Ermos, 2022

The right of Vashti Hardy and George Ermos to be identified as the
author and illustrator of this work has been asserted by them under the
Copyright, Designs and Patents Act 1988.

ISBN 978 0702 30256 5

Printed by CPI Group (UK) Ltd, Croydon, CR0 4YY
Paper made from wood grown in sustainable
forests and other controlled sources.

1 3 5 7 9 10 8 6 4 2

www.scholastic.co.uk

CHAPTER 1
PERFECT

The new year began with the sun in the sky and frost on the ground. Harley Hitch bounded into Grandpa Eden's greenhouse, jumped balletically over a large pot of seedlings, grabbed the hands of Daisy the greenhouse robot and danced a quick boogie, then cartwheeled through the strawberry patch towards Grandpa Eden.

"Whatever has got into you?" asked Grandpa Eden, laughing.

"I'm just getting it out of my system," Harley sang operatically, then pulled him into a squeeze.

"Getting what out of your system?"

"Me." She let go of Grandpa Eden, then pulled a silly face, and they both laughed.

"Why would you want to get yourself out of your system?"

"Because this is the term, Grandpa Eden."

"Yes, it's a new term."

"No, *the* term: I'm going to do it."

"Do what?" he asked suspiciously, his eyes narrowing. Harley had got into all sorts of knots when the Iron Forest was in peril last term. Everything had turned out all right in the end, but they still had a slightly oversized slug in a pen by the greenhouse to show for it.

"Pupil of the Term, of course! There's going to be no more chaotic Harley or wild schemes, no more exploding inventions or oversized gastropods: it's all perfect pupil from now on.

Professor Fretshaw will have to give me the golden light bulb pin this term." Harley had wanted to win Pupil of the Term ever since it had been introduced at Cogworks. She'd come close many times but was usually pipped at the post by her nemesis, Fenelda Spiggot.

Grandpa Eden nodded thoughtfully and stroked his peppery-grey beard. "It seems you've thought a lot about this."

"I've been thinking about it all through the holidays and there's no going back. In fact, Grandpa Elliot is ironing my new uniform right now."

"Would you like some help sewing on your pockets, and fixing your tool chains?"

She shook her head resolutely. "No adaptations this term, Grandpa Eden. Everything is going to be Cogworks-regulation perfect. I've even programmed Sprocket with a new setting."

Harley whistled and Sprocket, Harley's robot pet dog, bounded into the greenhouse and began jumping up at Harley enthusiastically. Rather than bending down and rollling around on the floor with him, or scooping him into her arms like she usually did, she calmly put a hand up and said, "Sprocket, play perfect."

In an instant, Sprocket stopped jumping, put his nose in the air, and started walking slowly in a circle and lifting his knees high, like a show horse.

Grandpa Eden laughed. "Well, as long as you know what you're doing."

"I do. Now, I need to polish my new shoes, then do some homework." There was no way Harley was going to risk Fenelda Spiggot scoring higher than her in any assignments this term.

"But school doesn't start until tomorrow? How can you have homework already? And new shoes? Aren't your boots much better for playing in?"

"I set the homework myself, and Professor Fretshaw never liked my boots, so I'm trying shoes." She shrugged. "I'll see you later, Grandpa. Come on, Sprocket."

"Before you go, Daisy has been working hard to get the blueberry bushes, woad and indigo plants ready. We should be able to make

7

a fabulous, vibrant blue dye for your hair this term."

"Ah … about that. I've changed my mind."

"You want to choose a different colour?" Grandpa Eden frowned. "It's a bit late notice, but I do have some beets which might make a rather striking pink dye."

"No, I mean I've changed my mind completely. I'm going back to my natural colour this term."

Sprocket gave an inquisitive yip.

"But you love changing the colour for each new term. It's your thing."

Harley gave a nod. It was her thing, and in truth she was itching to try the new blue, but she had to be perfect this term and blue hair didn't fit in with her plan. "Full regulation, Grandpa Eden."

Harley left the greenhouse imagining the golden light bulb pinned to her waistcoat.

Later that day, when she was satisfied that she'd completed enough homework, Harley decided to call for her friend Cosmo and head over to Rusty River. It had become one of their favourite places to hang out, and while Harley thought she had a solid plan for the term ahead, it wouldn't harm her to get a bit of extra advice from the ever-wise mechanical fish they could catch.

As they walked carrying their fishing poles, Harley noticed Cosmo kept giving her side glances. She paused. "What is it, Cosmo?"

"There's something different about you, Harley, but I can't put my finger on it."

Drawing herself up tall and lifting her chin,

Harley said, "Do I look more … Pupil-of-the-Term ready?"

Cosmo frowned and shuffled his feet in that way he did when he was confused. "I'm not sure what you mean."

Harley told him her perfect plan for the term and showed him Sprocket's new trick.

"Oh, I see. I suppose it could work." He bent down and patted Sprocket.

"Still no luck persuading your mum on getting a robot pet? It could be so fun. We could take them out for walks to the Iron Forest together."

"No chance, I'm afraid."

"Even after you won Pupil of the Term?"

Cosmo shrugged. "She says robots are for work, not play."

"Even after the new Rights for Robots bill?"

"Even after winning Pupil of the Term and even after the new robot rights bill." He sighed.

Soon, they reached Rusty River and cast their fishing lines.

Harley's line tugged almost immediately and she reeled it in. She had caught a long, slender metal pike, over a metre in length. Two large eyes stared at Harley from its narrow, tapered head. It opened its large, flattened snout to reveal a mouth full of sharp teeth. Cosmo jumped back and Harley almost dropped it.

"It's harmless, just big," she said, readjusting her grip and giving Cosmo a reassuring nod. She looked back at the pike. "I'm ready. Give me your best advice."

The metal pike cleared its throat. "Nothing is so certain as the unexpected." Then the fish backflipped out of her hands, completed a medal-worthy somersault, and disappeared back into the water with barely a splash.

"Did you hear that?" she breathed.

Cosmo frowned. "I wonder what that means?"

Her eyes glistened. "I know exactly what it means. No one expects me to win Pupil of the Term because there's usually some no-fault-of-my-own mishap."

"No fault of your own?" said Cosmo. "We'll not mention the giant slug, then." He coughed and laughed.

"All right, the occasional, overenthusiastic mishap, but you heard the fish. It means my be-perfect plan is on track." She wiggled her eyebrows.

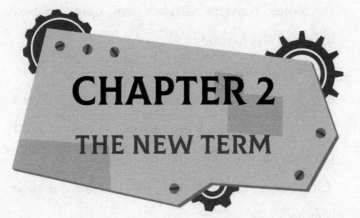

CHAPTER 2
THE NEW TERM

The next day, Harley arrived ten minutes early at Cogworks.

"Good morning, Primbot," she said brightly.

Primbot was a tall, thin robot who looked extraordinarily similar to the head teacher, Professor Fretshaw. "Harley Hitch, you're on time!" the robot said, sounding surprised.

Fenelda had just been dropped off by her

father in their fancy new transporter. As always, she looked flawless with her neat, blunt-bobbed hair and shiny shoes.

Keep your enemies close, Harley thought to herself. A fish had once told her that, and this term she wanted to play close attention to how well Fenelda was doing in all her schoolwork. "Good morning, Fenelda, did you have a nice holiday?"

As Fenelda spun around, Harley could tell she was poised to say something snide about Harley's appearance, as was customary with Fenelda. But Fenelda paused, looked her up and down, frowned, said, "Yes, thank you," then turned and went into the main Cogworks building.

Cosmo ran up the path to join Harley. "I'm not late, am I?"

Sprocket jumped up happily and Cosmo gave him a stroke.

"You will be late if you loiter here much longer," said Primbot.

After saying goodbye to Sprocket, Harley smoothed down her skirt, tucked her hair neatly behind her ears, tapped the golden light-bulb badge on Cosmo's waistcoat and said, "Don't you get too used to having that."

He tucked his curly, floppy fringe behind his ears. "Or, I might just win it again!" He smiled and they made their way up the path towards Cogworks.

The garden-bots were busily pruning and planting bulbs along the side of the path, and Harley was about to stop for a quick chat when she became aware of the tall, lean figure of Professor Fretshaw standing at the top of the Cogworks steps. The head teacher didn't approve of conversing on a friendly basis with the robots. Harley stopped herself and hurried up the steps. "Good morning, Professor Fretshaw," she said politely.

"Harley." Professor Fretshaw gave a nod and Harley caught her eyes brushing over her appearance and the hint of a quizzical frown.

Harley smiled to herself, then went inside and up the moving staircase to her classroom.

There was the vibrant buzz of chatter, the sort that always comes after a festive holiday. Letti was chatting with Asma, who had moved from another class and was showing Letti her new pencil case with many sliding compartments and secret tools. They both looked over and waved. Rufus was describing his new hover skates to Henry, which Harley thought sounded fun.

Professor Spark strolled into the room in her navy dress with stars all over it. "Good morning, class! Welcome back to a new term at Cogworks. If you can all settle down swiftly, I'll take the register, and we can begin what I believe is going to be a very exciting few months."

Harley sat up extra straight as Professor Spark called the names.

Narrowing her eyes, Fenelda turned around. "What are you up to? No wacky hair colour, no strange style with all your tools and usual paraphernalia?"

Despite the fact Harley was itching to bite back with a response, she ignored Fenelda, and looked straight ahead.

"Is everything all right, Fenelda?" asked Professor Spark, pausing the register.

"Oh, sorry, Harley was kicking the back of my chair and distracting me. I was telling her to stop."

A fuse lit inside of Harley. How dare Fenelda try to get her into trouble? This time she really was staying out of mischief!

Harley was about to blurt something defensive when Cosmo stood up. "Please, Professor Spark, Harley didn't do anything."

Professor Spark gave a nod. "Shall we try to start this term in the way we mean to go on?"

"I must have been mistaken," said Fenelda, glaring at Cosmo.

Harley whispered a thank you to Cosmo under her breath. She noticed his cheeks were a little flushed. He didn't like to draw too much attention to himself usually, so to do what he just did was a brave act. It felt good to have a friend like him beside her.

"Now the register is done, we've got some very exciting projects to complete this term, and Professor Fretshaw has told me to pass on that she'll be keeping a close eye on your assignment results for Pupil of the Term."

Harley leaned forward eagerly. If she could nail the first project, she'd be off to a good start.

"It's the spring term and the weather is still mild, so I've been thinking about the most efficient ways of keeping homes warm. Your project is about heat loss, so I'd like you to design and build a working model of an energy-efficient home and—" Professor Spark glared at Rufus, who was whispering to Tarak and delving in his bag. "Is there something you'd like to share with the class, Rufus?"

"Sorry, Professor. Someone handed me this flyer on the way to school."

Professor Spark held out her hand and Tarak took the flyer from his bag and passed it to her. Unfurling it, Professor Spark read,

**MONOCLES'
MARVELLOUS
MACHINES**
A CIRCUS ADVENTURE
OF A LIFETIME

**VISITING
FORGETOWN
SOON!**

She handed the flyer back to Rufus with a small smile.

A bubble of excitement swelled inside Harley, and a buzz of chatter filled the classroom until Professor Spark raised a hand.

"I know, it's very thrilling. In fact I think I may be as excited as you all are. The famous Monocle sisters are old friends of mine."

Harley wondered how Professor Spark knew the Monocle sisters. Perhaps she used to be in the circus? She could just imagine Professor Spark with her twinkly eyes and starry dresses flying around on a trapeze.

Professor Spark smiled and shook her head. "Now, I can see your imaginations are running wild, but I played the cello in their travelling orchestra when I was a student. Now they have a mechanical band, but it was fun, back in the day."

"Do you still play, Professor?" asked Tarak near the front, who was an excellent drummer.

"I do! In fact, I am part of a little string trio with Professor Horatio and Dr Orbit. But we are veering off course; back to schoolwork and our heat-loss project. I'd like you to work in pairs of your own choosing. This will be a homework task outside of lesson times, and you will have the first half of the term to complete the project. As for the winners, I shall be putting them forward with a high recommendation for Pupil of the Term."

This was it! Harley's chance. She looked at Cosmo and gave him a determined nod. She put the excitement of the circus out of her mind. Fun was too much of a distraction.

Later, when Harley and Cosmo were walking into town to get some books out of the library to help with their project research, they saw that posters for the circus had appeared all over town, and speculation was building about when it would arrive and where it might set up.

Cosmo paused by one of the posters in the window of Cosmic Sewing. "They're arriving next week. Do you know, Monocles' Marvellous Machines tours the whole of Inventia, but they've never been to Forgetown before! I can't wait; I never got the chance to go in Inventia City. I wonder what we'll see..."

Although it was like trying to contain lit fireworks in a tiny box, Harley took a breath and turned to Cosmo. "I can't go. I've got homework to do, the tests to revise for, the project to work on, my uniform to iron and—" She desperately wanted to go, but she couldn't take her focus away from her plan.

"What?" Cosmo frowned so deeply that his glasses slid down his nose and fell to the floor. "All right: who are you, and what have you done with Harley Hitch?"

"I told you, much as that Pupil of the Term badge looks spectacular on you, I want to give myself the best chance possible, and if Fenelda Spiggot wins it yet again she'll be insufferable. That means I have to be perfect. No jaunting about at the circus for new Harley."

Cosmo's shoulders sagged. "You're not even joking, are you?"

She shook her head.

They carried on walking with their piles of books. "I'm going to see if Cogmill Café has any iced buns," said Cosmo.

"I'll wait outside with Sprocket."

Across the square, Fenelda Spiggot had

just come out of Kitchen Imagine. She strolled across the square towards Harley. "I know what you're doing."

"Really," said Harley flatly.

"You're trying to steal Pupil of the Term from me by trying to be me!"

Harley baulked. "Nel, may I remind you that Cosmo is the reigning Pupil of the Term? You're not the only one who can follow the rules, you know." Trust Fenelda to think she was being copied. Harley could think of plenty of other orderly, rule-abiding pupils at Cogworks.

Fenelda gave a pinched smile that made Harley's blood boil. She didn't want to be like Fenelda; she just needed to show Professor Fretshaw she could be perfect.

"Why would I want to be like someone

who unfairly accuses their friend of cheating at a cogflower competition?" Fenelda and Harley had been friends for the first few years at Cogworks. Then, Professor Fretshaw had introduced Pupil of the Term. There had been a competition to see who could grow the tallest cogflower, and Harley had won ... until Fenelda's accusation. Then Professor Fretshaw had disqualified Harley.

"Your Grandpa Eden is the best horticultural expert in Forgetown, Harley, and you did use his super-grow potion when you super-sized a slug for the Iron Forest." She put her hand over her mouth and sniggered. "Doesn't that prove that I was right all along?"

Harley started counting to ten. Grandpa Eden always said: if your boiler is about to blow, hold your breath and count to ten. If it still

wants to boil, then you can let it out. "Friends trust each other, they don't try to get ahead of them by lying!" she blurted on ten.

Then Harley noticed that outside Picante's Pizza Parlour a few doors down, Professor Horatio was standing and watching them with a disapproving look. Harley hadn't meant it to come out quite so forcefully, but Fenelda had pushed her buttons.

Harley took a breath. That was exactly what Fenelda had been trying to do: taking every opportunity to upend Harley and stop her chances of winning Pupil of the Term!

Fenelda smiled wryly, turned on her heels, and walked away across the square.

"Are you all right?" asked Cosmo, stepping out of the café and passing Harley an iced bun. "What did Fenelda just say?"

"Nothing I couldn't handle," said Harley, taking an extra-large bite.

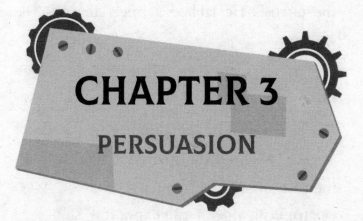

CHAPTER 3

PERSUASION

Cosmo wasn't about to give up on persuading Harley to visit the circus. She found flyers in her bag, on her doorstep, and Sprocket even had one in his mouth when he met her after school one day.

They were in their metalcraft lesson when Tarak let out a yelp of excitement.

"Whatever is it?" asked Professor Twine.

"Sorry, Professor, but I couldn't help it. It's the circus!" He jabbed a finger towards the window.

The class ran over. They were on a high floor, so the window had a sweeping view over the landscape. In the distance, a parade of brightly coloured transporters trailed in from the east towards Forgetown.

"It's really them!" said Cosmo.

Harley had to admit it was an extraordinary sight. Although it was hard to see the details from this distance, Harley could make out an enormous robot stomping slowly up the road. It held a red-and-gold banner, and behind it the troupe of colourful transporters glittered in the sun. Opening her mouth, Harley was about to say something excitedly to Cosmo … but clamped it shut again. She had the be-perfect plan to consider. If it had been any other term she would have been jumping for joy, but she'd committed to her strategy and it didn't include distractions, even if they were bright, shiny and oh so exciting.

"Opening night is going to be brilliant," said Cosmo.

"I'm sure you'll have a lovely time."

"Me? You mean you're still not going?"

"I have lots of work to get on with and I can't take an evening off."

Several expressions passed over Cosmo's face in a short time: he grimaced, then squinted, then laughed. "You're kidding, right? Nice one, Harley, I believed you for a moment."

"I'm serious. I'm committed to the be-perfect plan."

The colour drained from Cosmo's face and he turned back to watch the circus.

Harley put a hand on his shoulder. "Don't worry, you can go with Rufus, or Letti, or Tarak."

"No, you're my best friend and I want to go with you. How many times did I help you out last term?"

Harley sighed. If it wasn't for Cosmo, the last term could have turned out very differently, and no matter how much she wanted to do well this term, she would have probably been expelled if it wasn't for him. But could she risk taking her eye off the ball?

The sound of drums drifted towards them. The colours glimmered on the road, turning it into a rainbow.

"Look at it, Harley! Come on, you can take one day off from being the perfectly poised, studious Harley."

"Come along, class, that's enough excitement for one day," said Professor Twine. "I've got the results on your element naming test."

The class hurried back to their seats as Professor Twine walked about the tables giving back their papers.

"Good work, Henry, eighty per cent. Delores, fifty, you may need to go over yours again; Lettice, not bad, seventy; and … my, my, Harley, one hundred per cent! Excellent work."

Warmth filled Harley's chest.

Professor Twine continued handing back the papers. "Cosmo, ninety-five, great work. Fenelda, ninety-nine, excellent – you only missed one question!"

Fenelda's cheeks flushed red, her lips tightened, and she scowled.

Harley smiled quietly to herself. The term was going brilliantly. Getting one hundred in the test was a real boost, and the plans for the heat-loss project were going well. But Cosmo was her friend, and that was important too, as she'd found out last term when they'd fallen out. Perhaps it would be good to have a short break. Just for one evening. And she so wanted to go to the circus. She looked across at Cosmo, who was looking at her with puppy-dog eyes. "All right," she whispered. "I'll go, but just for opening night at the weekend."

Cosmo's face lit up.

When Harley arrived back at Hitch House after school, Grandpa Eden was wrestling with his wheelbarrow, which had a broken wheel.

"Oh, Harley, I'm glad you're back. Do you fancy a quick trip to the Iron Forest? The wheel pin has snapped, and I need to find a nailberry bush with a suitable replacement. We could take a wintery picnic, top Sprocket up with some hot cocoa and make an event of it when Grandpa Elliot gets home."

Harley's heart gave a little twist; she'd usually jump at the chance of a visit to the Iron Forest for a family picnic. They could see if the fuse-ferns were unfurling yet, search for the elusive velocipede in the common iron trees, perhaps collect a few silvercorns left over from the autumn…

She sighed. "I would love to, Grandpa, but I just promised Cosmo I would go to the circus with him at the weekend, so I need to get ahead with my schoolwork. I'd decided to give the circus a miss, but Cosmo can be very persuasive and I just got one hundred per cent in my elements exam, so I'm allowing myself just one treat."

"One hundred per cent in elements? That's brilliant! Seems your hard work is paying off." He paused and put a hand to his peppery beard. "But do you mean to say you were considering not going to the circus? That's unlike you."

Sprocket yipped robotically in agreement.

Harley was spared having to explain herself, as Grandpa Elliot had arrived home and walked into the greenwouse. "Hello! Did someone say circus? The newspaper wants someone to write a special on it, and of course I leaped at the chance!"

"We'll go on opening night on Sunday, just for an hour or so." Harley nodded.

Her grandpas exchanged a look.

"What?" asked Harley suspiciously.

"Are you sure you're not taking this Pupil of the Term thing too seriously?" said Grandpa Elliot. "You're working hard, which of course we approve of, but you've always worked hard in the past too. You don't want to burn yourself out."

"You do realize that a label and badge don't define who you are," added Grandpa Eden.

It was true, and she knew that deep down, but she had to try; she'd wanted Pupil of the Term for so long, and this new plan seemed to be working well. "I know, but I so want to win it, just once."

Grandpa Eden shrugged. "Well, as long as you know what you're doing. I'll pop to the Iron Forest while you do your homework."

"And I'll make us a hearty vegetable pie for dinner. You'll need lots of vitamins with all that work your brain is doing! Have you got some of those prize carrots, Eden?"

Harley made her way into Hitch House, closely followed by Sprocket. In the hallway he popped a ball out of his mouth so that it rolled in front of her. Powerball was usually their favourite game together. "Ah, you want to play?"

After throwing it once along the hallway for him to retrieve, she popped it into her pocket. "It's homework time, Sprocket. I promise next term we'll play every day after school."

He gave a disappointed whimper and followed her up the stairs.

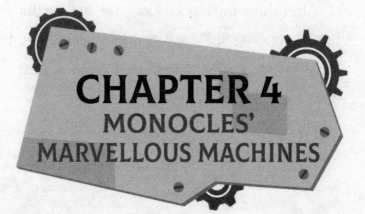

CHAPTER 4
MONOCLES' MARVELLOUS MACHINES

At the weekend, Harley insisted on working all of Saturday and most of Sunday in the library with Cosmo to get ahead with their schoolwork. With all the circus excitement, Professor Spark had set an optional bonus project to design a new circus act. Harley and Cosmo had come up with the idea of creating flame-juggling robots, which involved a lot of invention and mechanics, but Harley knew it would be quite spectacular if they managed to make it work. It was risky, as they would need to use liquid fire, which had caused them no end of trouble last term, so Harley triple-checked their calculations and design before returning home.

Sunday evening drew in, and, satisfied at their progress, Harley put on her favourite dungarees and star jumper and set off with her grandparents and Sprocket to collect Cosmo for the circus. It was sunset by the time they left, and the Moon rose above the Iron Forest, full and round, bathing the treetops in its silver light. The weather was crisp and fine, so they decided to walk rather than take the trundle bike.

They stopped off at Cosmo's house on Hinge Street. He answered the door wearing a rather brilliant midnight-blue velvet jacket and a bow tie with silver cogs.

"Very dapper!" declared Harley.

"I made one for Sprocket too." He handed Harley a matching bow tie.

"That's so sweet! Thank you. What do you say, Sprocket? Want to wear it?"

Sprocket's eyes lit with two red hearts. It was a recent upgrade that Harley and Grandpa Eden had made so that they could clearly see when Sprocket was happy. There was also a lightning option, but he'd not been mad enough yet to show those eyes.

After Cosmo put on Sprocket's bow tie, Sprocket leaped into Cosmo's arms and licked his face with his metallic tongue.

Mrs Willoughby peered disapprovingly over Cosmo's shoulder. "You won't be too late back, will you?"

"We'll return him safe and sound, don't you worry, Mrs Willoughby," said Grandpa Elliot.

"Thank you, Mr Hitch. I appreciate you taking him. He's spoken of nothing else for the past week." Cosmo's mum didn't approve of much, but Harley got the feeling Mrs Willoughby liked Grandpa Elliot. It was probably because he had a respectable job at the local newspaper.

"Come on, we don't want to miss the start!" Grandpa Eden ushered them out to the street and onwards to join the crowds of people heading out of Forgetown towards the circus.

Further along the path east, colourful tents looped with thousands of twinkling lights, and an enormous big top came into view, and Harley felt as though her stomach was suddenly full of fizzy lemonade bubbles. The giant robot

that Harley had seen strolling in when the circus arrived stood over the entrance, which was filled with people eagerly getting their tickets stamped. Twilight set in as they neared, making the lights all the more vibrant and magical.

"I feel I might burst with excitement!" said Cosmo.

"You're not the only one!" said Grandpa Eden, pointing at Grandpa Elliot's huge grin as he gazed up at the giant robot in wonder.

The Moon had moved higher in the sky, and the stars glittered brightly above, and Harley knew the stars would be watching keenly because they loved performances. In fact, there did seem to be an extraordinary number of stars out tonight, and they were growing more numerous by the second.

"Look!" Cosmo called at the same time that Harley realized the bright lights in the east weren't stars at all.

A fleet of drone eagles zoomed across the sky in formation heading towards them, their huge metallic bodies and feathered wings outstretched, rippling with lights. The crowd oohed and all eyes followed them as they rushed over the circus with a whooshing sound, took a full loop high into the sky, then criss-crossed so that their wings passed inches from each other.

"Incredible!" said Grandpa Eden. "Imagine the programming to get them to do that!"

"What are they doing now?" asked Harley, mesmerized by the drones as they circled and danced in the sky above the big top. "They seem to be forming letters! W-E-L-C-O-M-E!"

The crowd applauded as the lights of the drones rippled electric blue and ice white.

Harley, Cosmo, Sprocket and the grandpas reached the giant robot entrance, got their tickets stamped, then entered the circus site.

"We've got a bit of time before the main

show starts. How do you fancy visiting the Hall of Cyber Mirrors over there?" asked Grandpa Elliot, gesturing towards a silver tent. "I hear the mirrors can show you all sorts. We can see what we'd look like as robots – and robots can see what they would look like as humans!"

Sprocket barked enthusiastically, and they all dashed towards the entrance to the cyber mirrors.

Inside, glassy surfaces lined the edges of the tent, bent and curved in all sorts of ways. Harley stood before the first one and looked at her reflection. She was a round-headed robot the same height as herself with green-lit eyes, wiry hair and metal dungarees. When Harley grinned, the robot reflection grinned back. Suddenly a small fluffy white terrier was beside her robot reflection, and she realized Sprocket was standing beside her. Sprocket jumped upon seeing himself as a real dog, making Harley laugh as the dog in the mirror jumped and jumped along with him, sticking his tongue out of the edge of his mouth in the same way Sprocket did. Harley laughed.

She glanced to the side to see Cosmo marvelling at the metallic springs and golden glasses on the head of his robot reflection. Grandpa Elliot was doing some sort of robot dance with his reflection; Grandpa Eden was bent over in stitches watching.

After the cyber mirrors, they went back outside, and Grandpa Elliot treated them all to some candy clouds on sticks, then they hurried over to the carousel where shiny sailboats and glass seahorses rotated and bobbed on silver water which flowed around the inside. "I'm going on a seahorse!" called Harley.

"Me too!" said Cosmo.

As they rode the mercury waves of the carousel, Harley looked out to the crowds. Nearly everybody from Cogworks and the town seemed to be at the circus. Harley waved to Professor Spark, who was chatting with Professor Horatio and eating cog-shaped pretzels close by.

Letti and Tarak were watching a show not far away, where tiny wind-up figures acted out a play on a miniature stage, and Fenelda was climbing into the silver basket of a hot-air balloon designed like a planet, which rose a short distance above the site.

Soon, people began streaming into the big top.

"Come on! Time for the main event – we

need to get a good seat," said Grandpa Elliot.

Inside, many tiers of seats formed a horseshoe shape around a yellow sand central show area. Plush red curtains hung at the far end, which Harley assumed was where the acts entered and exited. They found seats near the front, and when the other benches were full, the lights dimmed, a spotlight shone on the red curtain, and the crowd fell silent.

A soft drum roll began, then grew in momentum. Everybody was on the edge of their seats. Two ladies in scarlet velvet jackets and long polished boots burst through the curtains and strolled out on to the stage.

"The Monocle sisters," called Grandpa Eden over the vigorous applause of the crowd.

The sisters were identical in every way, and had plaited dark hair under shiny black top hats, and their short jackets had long tails, brass buttons, and golden shoulder tassels.

They jogged along the edge of the stage, waving to the crowd, then looped back to the middle, took off their top hats, spread their arms wide to the audience and bowed. Their heart-shaped faces glowed and their smiles lit up the big top.

"Welcome to Monocles' Marvellous Machines, the greatest show in Inventia!"

"We are your ring-masters, Maria and Marissa Monocle."

"Let the magic of machinery begin!"

Above, huge metal bars and hoops descended, and a troupe of trapeze artists dashed on to the floor while the mechanical band struck up a raucous tune. They leaped like coiled springs up to the bars when they still looked impossibly out of reach.

"See their shoes?" said Grandpa

Eden. "Engineered with miniature rocket lift systems!"

"Wow, can we make a pair?"

The hoops and bars rose high again and began swinging and rotating in a complex pattern, then the trapeze troupe themselves spun and jumped in a dazzling display, moving as though they were dolphins in water.

Next, the Monocle sisters introduced the human butterfly, who at first looked as though she was just an ordinary person. Then, as she spread her arms, two enormous mechanical butterfly-like wings unfurled, rippling with light. An orchestra of self-playing instruments marched out to the stage and began performing a mesmerizing, magical tune. The human butterfly took off and flew around the tent in an airborne ballet.

Then came the blindfolded, rotating knife thrower, who threw a perfect pattern in the shape of a spanner on a target with lightning speed, then the acrobats balanced on top of each other to create the structure of a great common iron tree as tall as the big top.

"And now, ladies, gentlemen, children and robots! It's time for our most magical mechanical magician, a technology whiz capable of things we can only dream of."

Harley leaned forward, wondering if this magician needed an assistant. What a dream job that would be!

"What your eyes are about to witness is a feat of bending the space-time continuum, a blurring of the very fabric of the universe, a melding of dimensions."

Harley couldn't wait to see what was about

to happen.

"Monocles' Marvellous Machines gives you …
Elle Disappearo the Great!"

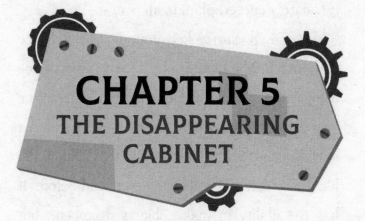

CHAPTER 5
THE DISAPPEARING CABINET

A woman with long, white, braided hair and dressed in a sweeping silver cape strolled through the curtains between the Monocle sisters. She was followed by a boy about Harley's age, dressed in a silver jacket and jeans. Behind them, several robots carried a large box-like object. They placed it in the centre of the stage. It was a tall, ornate cabinet with a mirrored door and engravings of constellations and intricately carved planets all over it.

Elle Disappearo looked around at the audience with her bright blue eyes. "Today you will see things that will seem unbelievable." Her voice was light and ethereal. "My marvellous cabinet is engineered with cutting-edge technology, the likes of which you will have never seen before. It has the ability to make objects disappear, but it does not merely hide them. Such is its power that it can teleport them to another world entirely. In fact, to another galaxy!"

The crowd gasped and Harley's mouth dropped wide open in amazement. "Teleporting to another world? Did you hear that, Cosmo?" It sounded like the most incredible thing Harley had ever heard. As far back as she could remember, she'd had the dream of creating a

transport that could fly her right up to the stars …
but imagine if she could simply teleport there!

The lights dimmed, and a large spotlight
illuminated the great cabinet, the magician and
her young assistant. Elle Disappearo took what
looked to be a large key from her pocket. When
she unlocked the cabinet, the door swung open
with an eerie creak. It was empty inside, and
looked like any ordinary cabinet. The boy stepped
inside, and Elle Disappearo closed the door.

"This mirror on this door is a screen which
will show us where the boy is in real time."

The crowd fell utterly silent. Elle Disappearo
turned the key three times clockwise with
dramatic extended motion of her arm in between
turns. On the third turn, electric sparks poured
out from hidden holes in the carved planets and
began spiralling around the cabinet. The crowd

oohed in delight. Then, with a flash of light, the sparks vanished. Elle Disappearo opened the cabinet door. The boy was gone.

"There'll be a secret door in the floor," whispered Grandpa Eden.

"But the cabinet is raised on feet!" Harley breathed.

"Shall we see where the boy has adventured to?" asked Elle Disappearo with a wry smile in Harley's direction.

Elle Disappearo shut the cabinet door. The mirror suddenly flashed and fizzled, then an image slowly came into view. It was the boy, but he wasn't in this world. He was bouncing around on the surface of what appeared to be another planet.

"Behold the images from another galaxy, where gravity is weaker and the boy now flies!"

He somersaulted and flew through the sky above blue grass and flowers the size of houses. The crowd looked on in wonder at what they were seeing. Harley wished she could swap places with the boy.

Then, after another bounce, the boy flew away from the land and over a hill. Enormous waves came into view, higher than the tallest common iron trees.

"Oh no! When the boy lands, he'll be done for!" said Grandpa Elliot.

The audience seemed to realize at the same time and let out a collective gasp. The boy tumbled towards the ocean.

But just as he was about to hit, Elle Disappearo was swift and turned the key three times anti-clockwise. The image faded and she opened the cabinet door. Inside, the boy stood dripping with water, but perfectly safe and well.

The self-playing instruments sang out two notes: *ta-dah!* And once more the audience cheered and cheered, no one harder than Harley, who thought it was the best thing she'd ever seen in her entire life.

After numerous bows, Elle Disappearo and the boy left the stage and the cabinet was wheeled away.

The Monocle sisters took to the stage once more.

"We hope you have all enjoyed the show this evening."

"But it's not over yet. If you all head outside there will be a final performance by the eagle drones, followed by a special cosmic-firework extravaganza!"

"Still want to leave early?" Grandpa Elliot winked.

"We may as well stay to the end." Harley smiled.

They hurried outside to watch as the eagle drones took flight and zoomed across the sky so fast they left colourful blades of light in the sky. Out of the corner of her eye, Harley saw the cabinet being wheeled into one of the small tents at the edge of the site. She couldn't stop thinking about it. What technology did it use to carry out such a breathtaking transportation? She looked over at the tent. She looked to the crowds of people.

Everyone was looking up, mesmerized by the drones. If Harley could get a closer look, she might be able to get a peek at the back of the cabinet where she suspected the tech would be, perhaps see a little of the mechanical workings that must have been hidden there. She looked down at Sprocket, who tilted his head curiously at her. She put a finger to her lips, took a couple of steps back, beckoned Sprocket to follow, then ducked out of the crowd and made for the tent.

CHAPTER 6
TOO MUCH OF A GOOD THING

Just as Harley was about to sneak inside, someone grabbed her arm.

"Where are you going?"

"Cosmo! I thought you were watching the drones." She peeled back a gap in the tent and peered inside. There were no people, just the cabinet surrounded by a variety of other gadgets and outfits on stands. "I want to get a closer look at the cabinet, perhaps see a little of how it works. Are you coming?" Before he could answer, she'd pulled him inside the tent.

Harley ran her hands around the edges of the cabinet. Close up, the carvings were beautifully detailed. "Look, the back panel seems to be thicker than the front; that must be where the technology is, but it doesn't appear to have an access panel anywhere."

"Harley, I'm not sure—"

"If we could get a quick look, maybe I could start designing one of my own. The workings are probably accessed from inside, if we could open the door to take a look, just for a moment."

"Ah, what a shame Elle Disappearo has the key and she's not about, so—"

"There's a gap! I don't think the door was locked properly!"

"Perhaps it's better if we—"

"If I put my finger here, and release this catch, and give it a little pull…"

The door had opened just an inch when there was a whirr and a thud. Sparks began flashing and whirling around the cabinet. Harley, Sprocket and Cosmo leaped back. With a bang, the door fell, lopsided, off its hinges. A puff of smoke chugged from the back of the box.

A ball of dread grew swiftly in Harley's belly. She clamped her hand to her mouth. What had she done? Sprocket whimpered. Something had gone terribly wrong. She'd broken the cabinet!

"You shouldn't have messed with it, Harley!" Cosmo said angrily.

"I think it's all right, probably just the hinges."

"Then what was that boom and all the sparks?"

"Perhaps we could mend the door quickly?" Frantically, Harley reached for her tool belt, then remembered she'd given up wearing her belt since she was trying to be perfect, so she didn't even have that. She looked around the tent for anything that might be of use.

A voice approached from outside. It sounded like one of the Monocle sisters. "Excellent show this evening. Well done, Elle. Such a wonderful finale to the main event."

"Thank you. I just need to wipe all the smoke residue from the cabinet, then I'll join the rest of the troupe to watch the fireworks."

Harley's stomach squeezed and Cosmo's eyes grew wide behind his glasses.

There was a horrible moment of indecision as their mouths dropped open. Should they stay and face what had happened, or run? Harley took a breath and braced herself. Then came a bang and the crackle-pop of the first firework.

"They've already started! Come on, you can clean it tomorrow. Let's celebrate a successful opening night."

Their voices faded and the bangs and crackles of fireworks continued.

"I should go after them and tell them what

happened," said Harley. She grabbed Cosmo's hand and pulled him out of the tent. But Elle Disappearo was already lost in the crowd.

"There you are!" called Grandpa Elliot. "We wondered where you were. I have to be up early for work, and you've got school in the morning, so we'd better head back. We'll still be able to see the fireworks from the road, and the circus is here for another week, so we can always come back one evening. I'll just grab Grandpa Eden."

Harley whispered to Cosmo, "It was only the hinges. I'm sure it can be fixed easily enough."

He nodded nervously.

"I'll go to the Iron Forest tomorrow, get more hinges, then sneak back here and mend it. No one but us will ever know."

Harley kicked herself that she'd even come

to the circus. She'd let her guard down, and of course something bad had happened – not the sort of thing that would help her win Pupil of the Term. "Everything will be fine, hinges are easy to mend, right?" she said to herself.

The grandpas returned, and they started walking towards the circus exit.

With a yawn, Grandpa Elliot said, "I think that was enough excitement to last me a whole year!"

"It's been fun, but you can have too much of a good thing, don't you think?" Harley gave a nervous laugh and paused to look over her shoulder in case she could spot Elle Disappearo. Cosmo shuffled nervously from foot to foot. With a sigh to herself, Harley resolved that her sensible self would resume with immediate effect. That was too close to disaster.

"We'll take you back home on the way, Cosmo." Grandpa Eden smiled.

Cosmo nodded. "Yes, thank you. I'm very tired." He shot Harley an angry glare.

Grandpa Elliot looked between the two of them with a curious expression. "You're both behaving a bit strangely all of a sudden." He looked down at Sprocket, who began his play-perfect routine.

Grandpa Eden shrugged, and they left the circus and made their way up the path towards Forgetown, the brilliance of the lights fading the further they went. After dropping Cosmo to his door, they followed the dark path back to Hitch House.

They weren't far when there was a thud.

"Oof!"

"Grandpa Elliot?" Harley felt around on the ground for her grandpa and helped him up.

"I'm fine, thank you. There must've been a rock on the path. I didn't see it."

"We should have brought the trundle bike, it has a headlamp," said Grandpa Eden.

"It does seem extra dark this evening," said Harley. "Sprocket, could you go full beam, please?" Sprocket's eyes lit up and projected two beams of light on the path ahead. "The Moon was bright earlier, so thick clouds must have blown in and covered it up."

They carried on back to Hitch House, although Harley couldn't help but wonder why, if there was a lot of sudden cloud, she could still see so many stars.

CHAPTER 7

LOST THINGS

"Has anyone seen my new trowel?" Grandpa Eden called from downstairs. "I was rather hoping to use it this morning to plant my bulbs."

"Afraid not, Grandpa, I'm still looking for my school tie."

"I must have put it in the wash last night. Sorry," called Grandpa Elliot from across the hall. "We were back so late from the circus I wasn't really thinking."

Harley scrambled around in her drawer. "It's OK. I'll wear my old tie."

"What's the time, Harley? I can't find my pocket watch."

She glanced at the clock on Sprocket's side. "Eight fifteen."

"Already!" said a panicked Grandpa Elliot. "But I feel like we've only just got up! We must have overslept." He dashed down the stairs, called out a goodbye and left for work.

Harley wanted to get back on track with her plan to be perfect, so although she still had forty-five minutes before school started, she grabbed a breakfast muffin from Grandpa Eden, called Sprocket, and left for Cogworks. Being early never hurt!

But when they reached the school gate, there

seemed to be a rush of pupils running for the door.

"What in all of Inventia is going on, Sprocket?"

Sprocket gave a confused whimper.

Asma ran past. "Come on, Harley! We're all going to be late! Haven't you seen the time?"

She pointed frantically at the Cogworks clock.

Harley looked up. It was almost nine o'clock.

"Sprocket, there must be something wrong with our clocks at home, because we left with plenty of time. Either that, or the Cogworks clock is wrong."

Sprocket barked and pointed to the clock on his side with his tail. It read almost nine o'clock too.

"How strange. We didn't stop, and we weren't walking slowly…"

Fenelda Spiggot barged past. "Hey, watch where you're going, Harley!"

"You watch where—" Harley stopped herself. Perfect Harley would rise above it.

Harley gave Sprocket a quick pat on the head. "I'd best hurry inside too. See you later, wonder pup!" And with that she pelted up the path behind Fenelda and into the building just as the clock struck nine.

To her surprise, Dr Orbit – who rarely left the star-chatter observatory – was in the entrance hall talking with Professor Fretshaw.

"It was most irregular, Professor Fretshaw. One moment it was there, and the next it had disappeared."

"There's likely to be a totally rational explanation. Clouds can seemingly appear from nowhere, as you know, and there were patches around last night. Perhaps the stars distracted you."

Dr Orbit tilted his head in thought. "Well, they did seem in a rather flamboyant mood – more than usual, at least – with all the fireworks going off. But it really does seem to be lost… It's usually very regular in its sky pattern."

Just as Harley was wondering what Dr Orbit

was talking about, Professor Fretshaw noticed her and turned with her hands on her hips. Harley froze, wondering if she had blown the be-perfect plan by being a minute late, but as there were still pupils streaming in through the doors, gasping for breath, she hoped not.

Professor Fretshaw narrowed her eyes. "I hear you got one hundred per cent in your elements test with Professor Twine."

"Yes, Professor."

Professor Fretshaw looked over Harley as though there were words printed on her uniform and she was trying to read them, then said, "Hm. Run along to class."

Harley wasn't sure if the professor's look was approving or mistrusting, but she decided to go with approving so smiled to herself as she hurried up to the steps.

Professor Spark dashed along the hall beside them in her midnight-blue dress speckled with stars. Her curly hair looked like it had been hurriedly tied up in a messy bun. "Come along, everyone! Settle down quickly! We all appear to be running late, probably due to the excitement of the circus last night."

The pupils took their seats and Professor Spark had barely finished the register when something hit the window beside Henry. He let out a yelp.

"Whatever is the matter?" asked Professor Spark.

"He's scared of a moth," Rufus laughed, pointing at the windowsill outside.

"Poor thing must be disorientated." said Professor Spark, opening the window. She scooped up the moth and put it on the plant on her desk. "I'll let it recover here and return it outside later."

She'd barely handed out the lesson's work when the bell rang to signify the next lesson. The class exchanged confused glances.

"How strange; the bell must be faulty," said Professor Spark. After looking at her digi-pad, she shrugged and said, "I must have been talking longer than I realized. You'd better all get off to your next lesson."

On their way to recycling craft with Professor Maple, Harley and Cosmo walked behind Fenelda, who was talking with Delores – loudly, as usual. "Did you hear the rumour that Dr Orbit lost something very important this morning?"

Delores said she hadn't.

"I don't know what it was, but it must be valuable."

"It's true, I heard him telling Professor Fretshaw this morning," Harley whispered to Cosmo. "I wonder what it is."

Fenelda continued, "There's something strange going on, because I wore my best necklace to the circus last night, and this morning I couldn't find it anywhere. It's very expensive. My parents will be mad if I don't find it."

"It's not quite the same, but I couldn't find one of my socks this morning," said Delores.

Cosmo and Harley stifled a giggle at the lost sock, but Harley did think it was a little strange that items had gone missing in Hitch House that morning too.

They reached Professor Maple's room and had just begun sorting through the recycling, ready to create self-portrait sculptures, when the bell rang for lunch.

"Wow, time's flying today." Harley shrugged, and they hurried to the lunch hall.

Cosmo chased the food around his plate.

"Are you going to eat that, or play robo-cat and mouse with it?" asked Harley.

"I'm not that hungry, to be honest. I feel as though I only just had breakfast."

"I'll have yours. I only had time to take a bite out of a muffin this morning." Harley gobbled up her food and was about to take Cosmo's spanner-shaped fries when the bell went again.

The entire lunch hall groaned.

"We haven't even had our outside break yet," said Cosmo. "Why is today being so weird?"

"Probably just a blip in the school bells. Or perhaps Professor Fretshaw is training us to be more efficient, to be sure we squeeze even more learning into the day?" Harley joked, taking a quick bite of one of Cosmo's fries. Then they both hurried to their next lesson.

Before they knew it, the bell rang for the end of the school day. Usually, everyone's robot pets met their children at the school gates, but when they got outside, no one was there.

"Where's Coppertail?" asked Letti, deflated. Her rabbit robot was usually bouncing with joy to see her.

"There's no sign of Awk either," grumbled Rufus.

"Or Slither," said Delores.

"Maybe Sprocket's helping Grandpa Eden." Harley frowned and started walking down the path with Cosmo. A strong gust of wind hit them and Harley had to fight to stay on her feet for a moment.

"That was weird," said Cosmo, picking up his glasses, which had blown right off his face.

"Maybe there's a bit of bad weather coming." Harley shrugged.

They had just reached where the road split when Sprocket bounded up the road and leaped into her arms. "I don't know if you're late, or if I'm early," said Harley as he licked her cheek apologetically. "I'll see you tomorrow, Cosmo."

"Er, yeah…" Cosmo said distractedly, looking at the sky, which had suddenly become the deep blue-grey of dusk.

"That's funny. It's darker, but there are no clouds. What's going on?" Harley asked. The day was becoming more curious by the moment.

"I don't know, but I'm going to be late home and Mum will be worried. See you tomorrow, Harley!"

Then they dashed up their respective paths home.

As Harley came within view of Hitch House, Grandpa Elliot pulled up in the tri-wheel trundle bike. "You're late back from school. Did Professor Fretshaw keep you behind?"

She shook her head. "No, you're back

from work early."

He frowned. "I still can't find my pocket watch, but the clock at work definitely said it was time to leave. I had to rush my write-up on the lost tide."

"Lost tide?"

"Yes, the strangest thing happened at the south coast between Forgetown and Inventia City: there was no high tide! I've written an article on it which will appear in the *Forgetown Daily* tomorrow."

Of all the lost things she'd heard rumours of today, that seemed to be the strangest.

When they reached the house, Grandpa Eden was outside staring up at it.

"Are you all right, Grandpa Eden?"

He smiled. "Yes, I'm fine. But look! There are buds on our trailing roses! They shouldn't be out until the summer." He shook his head, puzzled. "Any sign of your pocket watch, Elliot?"

"None at all. I'd have another look, but I should probably get dinner ready. Chuck-in-the-oven pizza for dinner, everyone? There's not really time for anything else."

"Sounds good to me," said Harley. She suddenly remembered she should have gone to the Iron Forest to get the new hinges after school, but the day had taken a strange turn and distracted her. It was too late to go now. "I'll go straight to my room. I've mountains of schoolwork to complete and, judging by how the day has gone, only about half an hour until bedtime."

Up in her room, Harley tried her best to focus on her work, but Sprocket kept looking out of the window, whimpering. "What is it, wonder pup?"

She joined him. The stars were bright in the night sky. Dr Orbit popped into her mind. What had he been talking to Professor Fretshaw about that morning? What had he lost? She gazed out at the deep blue sky.

Like a bolt of electricity to her chest, she realized what it was.

There was no Moon.

CHAPTER 8

TIME FLIES

It had clearly been a full moon the night before, yet this evening there was nothing there.

Swiftly, Harley ran and took her transmitter from her bag. "Cosmo! Cosmo, are you there?"

After a moment he answered. "Yes. I'm in bed."

"Sorry, did I wake you?"

"No. Mum insisted it was bedtime, but I'm

not remotely tired. I feel as though I've only just got back from school!"

"Cosmo, look out of your window."

"Harley, if you're on our driveway…"

"Don't be daft, I'm at Hitch House. Look at the sky."

"I'm looking."

"What can you see?"

"Er … sky … stars… What are you getting at?"

"I'll rephrase it. What can't you see?"

After a pause, Cosmo said, "Where's the Moon? Wait, let me look out of the window on the other side… It's not there either!"

"Right?"

"It's as though it's vanished into thin air!"

Harley's stomach twisted. The magician's cosmic cabinet rolled through her mind.

"When we were walking back after the circus, it became so dark that Grandpa Elliot tripped over. We didn't think anything of it at the time, but … when we left for the circus, the Moon was out, but by the time we left it had gone."

"So are you saying you think the Moon's been missing since last night?"

"Exactly! And today, so many other things have gone missing too. I … I don't think it's a coincidence. Something happened yesterday evening."

"Harley?"

It was all becoming clear. The extraordinary power of the cabinet. Her mishap with it…

"The cosmic cabinet. When I broke it, that's when things started disappearing. I think all of this is my fault!"

By the time Harley got to sleep, it was time to get up again. Sprocket licked Harley's face.

"Urgh, I'm too tired," she said.

He barked, urging her to wake up.

"It can't be morning already." She hauled herself out of bed and went to the kitchen for breakfast. Grandpa Elliot was dashing out of the door.

"Why are you off so early?" Harley rubbed her eyes.

"The *Forgetown Daily* sent a transmission to leave early. There are a couple of strange stories coming in. Another confirmed high-tide failure and reports that the same has happened all around the coast of Inventia. And brace yourself for something odd, but apparently there are rumours that the Moon has gone missing! They want to run an urgent feature before the *Inventia City Times*."

"It's really missing?" Harley had hoped last night's revelation had been a bad dream. "It seems impossible."

"Right? Gone in a puff of smoke, as easy as that magician at Monocles' made the boy disappear in her cosmic cabinet!"

Harley let out a nervous laugh.

"I'd put it down to the weather, but last night was clear as glass. Apparently, no one has seen the Moon since early Sunday evening."

Grandpa Eden came down the stairs, yawning.

"I'd better get to school," said Harley. She needed to speak to Cosmo again and decide what to do.

"Don't forget your coat," said Grandpa Elliot.

Sprocket popped up his temperature gauge.

It read "Weather – warm".

"Sprocket says I won't need one."

"Of course you will! It's barely February," said Grandpa Elliot.

"Yet the roses are in full bloom," said Grandpa Eden, pointing out the window.

Grandpa Elliot scratched his head. "What in all Inventia is that all about?"

"Have you found your pocket watch yet?" Harley asked tentatively.

"No. It seems to have vanished along with the Moon! I'll look again just as soon as I have time." And with that he dashed out the door.

As Harley approached Cogworks, Primbot was standing with her head in her hands. "I can't keep up! One moment everyone is early, then they're late. I give up." Harley hurried by, and couldn't help a small smile.

Cosmo waved and ran to join her.

"What are the garden-bots doing?" asked Harley, looking over at them flying around the borders.

"There's been a sudden growth spurt, as though it's summer all of a sudden. It's the same in town."

"And what's that every-help-bot doing up the ladder?" Harley pointed to the robot climbing up to the Cogworks clock.

"Professor Fretshaw's orders, I heard. Around a thousand silver-wing moths have decided to make the clock their new home," said Cosmo.

Sprocket barked and pointed to his clock.

"Almost nine o'clock? Thanks, wonder pup. See you after school."

Once inside, all the pupils were ushered into the hall for an urgent assembly. Professor Fretshaw addressed the pupils: "My glasses have disappeared…"

"Hardly as pressing as the missing Moon,"

Harley whispered to Cosmo.

"…Professor Horatio has lost his violin, and several students have reported missing items as well. If anyone else has lost any items, you are to report it to me today. We are very much hoping there isn't a thief in our midst."

"Seems a bit strange," Fenelda whispered to Letti from the row in front of Harley. "They should interrogate anyone who's been acting very peculiar lately" Harley leaned in to listen.

"Lots of things have gone missing since the circus came to town. Does anyone even know who these Monocle sisters are? They could be arch criminals! It can't be a coincidence that my expensive necklace went missing that same night. Perhaps they distract us with their fireworks, and that's when they strike…"

Harley glanced at Cosmo and frowned. She

didn't like the idea of accusing the Monocle sisters when there was no evidence at all. And there was the fact that she was pretty sure that there was no thief. She'd broken the cabinet, and the Moon and other objects had all disappeared at the same time.

After the assembly was dismissed, Harley pulled Cosmo to one side. "I feel terrible. Why didn't I just own up to breaking the cabinet at the time? This is all my fault."

"There's no way you could have known what happened. It just … broke a little."

"Even so. I should have faced up to it straight away. I even meant to repair the hinges, but then time started being weird."

Cosmo twisted his mouth uncomfortably.

"My grandpas are going to be so disappointed."

"They'll understand. Your grandpas are the best."

"That's what makes it even harder, that I've done this. I've got to go back to the circus straight after school and tell them what I did … and just hope that Elle Disappearo can help me bring everything back."

"How about the hinges to mend the cabinet?"

Harley pulled a miniature version of Sprocket out of her waistcoat pocket. She held it in her palm and pressed the nose, which lit green. "Sprocket, could you go to the Iron Forest and collect a variety of the strongest-looking hinges from the rusty willow, please, and bring them to me after school?"

The tiny model Sprocket let out a mechanical bark.

"Thanks, buddy." She depressed the nose and put it back in her pocket.

"Are you going to tell your grandpas before going?" asked Cosmo.

She shook her head. "It was my mistake. I need to take responsibility. Besides, with time flying, I should go straight there. I need to make sure it's sorted before Fenelda spreads the rumour that the Monocles are thieves any further." Once more Pupil of the Term had become like sand slipping through her fingers.

"Do you want me to come with you?"

"No. You tried to stop me, and you'll just get caught up in it all again." She took a breath. "It's best if I face it alone."

CHAPTER 9

OWNING UP

As soon as the school bell had rung, Harley met up with Sprocket outside and ran with him to the circus site, which was hard at times because odd gusts of wind kept slowing her down.

The circus camp was quiet. It didn't seem like anyone was preparing for their next performance that evening.

"Hello, how can I help you?"

Harley hadn't noticed one of the Monocle sisters beside one of the tents, tuning a self-playing instrument. She looked at her with golden-brown eyes. Her skin was smooth as polished stone and Harley suddenly quite star-struck to be so close to one of the ringmasters.

"Excuse me for interrupting, Miss Monocle, but may I have a word with Elle Disappearo?"

The Monocle sister observed her for a moment, then nodded in the direction of one of the tents. "She's in there."

Harley lingered, thinking how strange it was that no one seemed to be busying about getting ready for a show. "Isn't there a performance this evening?"

"We did plan to, but then time went astray, and the rumours started."

"Rumours?" Harley's shoulders tensed, wondering if Fenelda's theory had got around.

"It seems a lot of people have lost things, and they want to point the finger at us." The Monocle sister raised her eyebrows.

"That's not fair," said Harley, her stomach twisting.

"No, but we can't stop what people are saying."

"I'd better go and speak with Elle Disappearo, if that's all right." Harley walked over to the tent. She raised her hand to knock but realized that wouldn't quite work on the fabric. "Hello?" She poked her head through the gap to see Elle tinkering with the broken door of the cabinet along with the other Monocle sister sorting through a tool box.

Looking over her shoulder, Elle smiled.

"Come on inside. What can I do for you?" She wore a red jumpsuit and her silver-blonde hair fell in waves to her waist.

"I'm so sorry to disturb you, but the other night when I came to the circus, I did something I shouldn't have."

"Go on."

The other Monocle sister glanced over.

Harley drew a deep breath. "After your show – which was marvellous, by the way, the most impressive thing I've ever seen. In fact, I loved it so much that my curiosity got the better of me." Her cheeks burned as she prepared to admit her mistake. "I sneaked into your tent, just to get a closer look. I love mechanics and inventions and anything to do with space and other worlds, and I thought I might be able to see how you did it."

"A conjuror never reveals her secrets."
Elle winked.

"I shouldn't have, but I touched the door and the sparks went off and… It was me who broke the cabinet. It's all my fault."

Elle Disappearo frowned.

The other Monocle sister entered the tent. "Have you seen the winding tool, Maria?" She looked at Harley and Elle. "Is everything all right?"

"I was just telling Elle that I accidentally broke her cabinet, but it's not just that." She licked her lips nervously. "I must've done something really bad and unleashed its power somehow, because that's when everything disappeared. The Moon, all the objects that have gone missing, the things you're being blamed for … it's all my fault." Harley braced herself.

The Monocle sisters looked at each other, then to Elle Disappearo, then they all looked at Harley.

And smiled.

"Dear thing, you'd better have a seat, then we'll explain a few things to you." Elle Disappearo pulled up a chair for her.

"We understand curiosity. We embrace it at Monocles'," said one of the sisters. Standing beside each other, Harley couldn't tell which sister was which. Even the way they stood with a hand on one hip was the same. "Much of what we do is cutting-edge technology and invention, but some of it is pure trickery."

"But not the cabinet!" cried Harley. "I saw it with my own eyes, and it must be more powerful than even you realize if it can make the Moon disappear."

Elle shook her head. "The cabinet is a machine of illusion."

Harley couldn't make sense of what she was hearing. "But … the pictures of the boy in another world looked so real!"

"Simulated imagery, pre-recorded. It is rather convincing, isn't it?" said Elle.

"It doesn't really send things to other worlds?"

Elle shook her head. She opened the cabinet. "See? There's a false door at the back. The boy squeezes inside, and then when I open it, he appears to have vanished. It's rather convincing to the audience because their eyes are so focused on the wonders they are seeing onscreen. The mind wants to believe it, so it does."

"But the boy was wet from the waves!"

"A simple pod of water he keeps in his pocket to break at the appropriate time. And the hinges were about to break anyway; they'd become rusty, and I had been meaning to replace them. When your curiosity got the better of you, you were just unlucky."

"So, I didn't break it?" Harley wasn't sure whether to feel relief or more confusion.

"When you opened the door, the hinge failed, and the bump must have set off the explosions that are triggered when I turn the key. No harm done. But I appreciate you owning up to it."

"But if the cabinet didn't break and make things disappear, then where have they gone?"

"That's a mystery we can't answer," said one of the sisters. "We wish we could, because our reputation is being tarnished – and we need our reputation to bring in crowds. So we've decided to pack up and leave before things get any worse."

It annoyed Harley that people leaped to

conclusions about the circus rather than investigating. People just came up with a lazy answer to the missing objects. "Please, you can't go! I need a chance to put things right."

"But whatever has happened to the missing objects and the Moon, it was never your fault. It's not down to you to make it right."

Even so, things were in chaos, and nobody seemed to know what to do. Harley had to try.

"It's not right that people are blaming you. Can you give me a few days to at least try?"

"The people of Forgetown don't want us here any more."

"Just a few days. Please?"

They looked between each other.

"All right. It's quite clear someone has to get to the bottom of this. If we can help, you only need to ask."

"Thank you, I will."

"Where will you start?"

After a moment of thought, Harley shrugged. "I guess I should start with the biggest missing object: the Moon."

CHAPTER 10
THE MYSTERY OF THE MISSING MOON

The first thing Harley did when she got back to Hitch House was to explain everything that had happened to her grandpas.

"You see, I thought it was my fault, but the cabinet didn't make the objects go, so something or someone else must be responsible."

"You shouldn't have messed with the cabinet," said Grandpa Elliot, giving her one of his disapproving looks.

"I know, I'm sorry."

"But, in the grand scheme of this week, that's the least of our worries. Not only are things missing but there is the alteration in time, the strange behaviour of the weather and the tides, and the moths at Cogworks."

"I agree," said Grandpa Eden. "But I think I have the answer to part of the mystery."

They leaned in.

"I was thinking about the roses appearing, and the other curious things today, when it struck me that the tides, the length of the day, the seasons, the high winds, the moths, they're all linked to the presence of the Moon. Without it they go out of balance. The pull of its gravity keeps the planet's rotation slower and gives us the tides. It keeps the planet at a certain tilt affecting the seasons, and moths are guided by its glimmer."

"Of course! That makes sense now you say it." Harley couldn't believe she hadn't thought of it. "The Moon is at the centre of this: find the Moon thief first and we solve the biggest problem, and it will hopefully lead us to find everything else."

The grandpas nodded in agreement.

"Who would steal the Moon, and what motive would they have?"

"Money?" suggested Grandpa Eden.

Grandpa Elliot thought for a moment, then said, "If it was money, then they would have come forward with their demands by now, surely? Why delay?"

"Then who?" asked Harley, searching her mind for possible answers. "And how? It must have been someone with a lot of resources.

Are there any powerful inventors in the city who would have reason to cause a lot of chaos?"

Grandpa Elliot shrugged. "I can't think how anyone would benefit from what's going on."

As they sat and thought, the clock struck midnight.

"Let's all sleep on it," yawned Grandpa Eden. "We might have fresh ideas in the morning."

It was impossible to sleep with all the thoughts and questions buzzing around in Harley's brain, so she sent Cosmo a transmission to update him on what had happened.

She decided to make a list of suspects when her transmitter bleeped and Cosmo came into view.

"Sorry, I meant for you to pick up my

transmission message in the morning. Did I wake you?"

"It is the morning."

"Oh, cricket! Then I'd better get ready for school. Can you leave early and meet me at the crossroads? Then we can chat on the way."

At the crossroads, Harley was already waiting when Cosmo arrived. She handed him her list, which he read aloud as they walked: "A master criminal escaped from prison, one of the stars, and Fenelda. That's a pretty odd list."

"I'm struggling with motives, to be honest. Do you have any ideas?"

"How about you tell me why you've come up with these three."

"A master criminal, because they might want money in exchange for the return of the stolen objects. Grandpa Elliot says it's unlikely because they would have asked for a ransom by now, but we can't rule it out."

"Good thinking. OK, what about the stars?"

"This is a tricky one because the stars are fabulous. But they do share the sky with the Moon, so for that reason, they're on the list. Maybe they thought the Moon was too bright, that they would shine brighter without it?"

"Hmm, that's grabbing at straws, but we haven't got much else to go on. And Fenelda?"

"Because she's the one who started the rumours suggesting the circus are behind it. It might be a clever diversion tactic. And because, you know, she's Fenelda."

"I suppose the rumour is suspicious. What do we do next?"

"Interview the suspects. Bearing in mind we don't actually have a specific person in mind as our escaped criminal, I say we start with Fenelda and then the stars."

"We should interview everybody who lost something too, in case they have a clue."

"Good idea!"

They reached the school gates. "I'll interview the two main suspects and you start on the lost object group," said Harley. It felt good to have a plan.

Up ahead, Fenelda stepped out of a

transport and hurried up the steps.

"No time like the present," said Harley, giving Sprocket a quick pat goodbye and running after her.

"Nel, wait!"

"If you want to work with me on the school project, the answer is no."

"Er, that's not it. I just wanted to see how you were, after losing your necklace. It must be very worrying."

Fenelda narrowed her eyes.

"But you can't really think the circus is behind it. They're such lovely people."

Fenelda ignored her, turned, and continued walking into the main Cogworks building.

"Your necklace must be a big loss, but really it's nothing compared to the Moon going missing."

"Not really; who cares about the Moon?" she called.

"And when did you last see your necklace, and the Moon, for that matter?"

With a loud sigh, Fenelda stopped. "Harley, what are you doing? Do you think solving this is going to get you Pupil of the Term or something?"

"Not at all. I'm just trying to get to the bottom of it and stop the circus being blamed."

"Suit yourself. And while you're focusing on playing detective, I'll be beating you in every test from now on." Fenelda stepped on to the moving staircase.

Cosmo caught up with Harley. "I just asked Professor Fretshaw if she'd found her glasses and she said no."

"That doesn't help much."

"She remembered giving them to Primbot to clean, and then taking them to the circus with her, but she hasn't seen them since."

The bell rang for the start of school. "We need to keep an eye on Fenelda," Harley said. "She's acting suspicious."

"In what way?"

"Just her usual Fenelda way." Harley wasn't sure, but after what Fenelda had said, she wouldn't put it past her that she was doing it all as a big distraction to divert Harley from winning Pupil of the Term. "Come on, let's get to class. I'll speak to the stars at the end of the day."

CHAPTER 11
INTERVIEWING
THE STARS

At dusk, the star-chatter observatory glistened on the opposite hill to Cogworks. Harley loved the beautiful glass-domed building and her star friends. She was feeling bad that she'd been so busy with her be-perfect plan she'd not been to visit them since the holidays.

She climbed the spiral steps with Sprocket and saw Dr Orbit at the telescope.

"Harley! We've rather missed you these past few weeks. The stars keep asking me when you're next visiting, but I told them you're very busy with your schoolwork."

"Hello, Dr Orbit. Sorry I've not been about much. May I take the west telescope?"

"Of course."

She sat in the seat of the large telescope pointing west. It felt nice to be back. She moved the telescope across the vast beauty of the evening sky, tracking her coordinates carefully until she saw Ursa Major, flamboyant in her all-white ball gown, with lots of sparkle and feathers.

"Harley, dahr-ling!" Ursa exclaimed when she saw her. "It's been too long. We've all missed you terribly. Oh, Proximaaaaa!" she sang out across the night sky. "Come quickly, sweetie pops. Look who's here!" Proxima appeared in a dazzling cerise diamanté dress.

"Harley, how are you? Mwah, mwah."

"Hi, Proxima. I love your new dress. The colour suits you."

"Thank you. It's for our new show we've been rehearsing. It's called the *Star Shimmer Cabaret*. It's going to be the most glorious event in the history of everything."

A third star joined them. "Did I hear someone say Harley was here?" It was Vega in his customary blue fur coat and elaborate headdress. "It is you! Do say you'll help us with our new show? When you helped direct the *Collapse of the Red Giant*, it was the most moving piece of the millennium. There wasn't a dry eye in the house. But wait... What's happened to your hair?"

"Oh,

nothing, I just

didn't dye it this term."

"My, you must have been as busy as Dr Orbit told us, you poor thing. You look like you need a bit of dazzle. Can we sprinkle some stardust on you? Perhaps some glitter gold? Perhaps we can we send down a feather boa or two?"

"Thank you, that's very kind of you, but I'm actually here on an important matter. Something that I hope you can all help with."

"Just say the word, Harley dahr-ling," said Ursa.

"Something important has gone missing from the night sky."

The stars looked between each other.

"Proxima, have you lost your favourite tiara again?" asked Ursa.

"It's not that, it's the Moon," said Harley. "It hasn't been seen since Sunday evening."

The stars frowned and looked blankly at her.

After a moment of silence, Vega cleared his throat. "What's ... the Moon?"

"Are you being serious?" Harley tilted her head, thinking he was probably joking with her.

"The Moon," said Ursa thoughtfully. "It sounds strangely familiar, but I can't place it."

"Seriously?" Harley said doubtfully. "The

Moon, as in the huge, rocky natural satellite that revolves around this planet."

With jazz hands, Proxima exclaimed, "I know! That strange, shape-shifting thing that lurks over the Iron Forest sometimes and blocks our view."

"Er, yes, that's the one." Harley couldn't believe it hadn't been instantly obvious.

"You're right," said Ursa. "I do believe we know what you mean."

"Missing, you say?" asked Proxima.

Harley nodded. "Last seen before the Monocles' Marvellous Machines' opening night.

"Oh, what a marvellous show that was," said Ursa.

"The fireworks!" said Proxima.

"The splendour!" said Vega.

Harley coughed. "Anyway, about the missing moon. Do you remember seeing it that night?"

The stars frowned and looked around, as though the answer might fall from the sky. After an excruciating few moments of silence Proxima said, "Actually, I believe I do remember seeing it. I was trying to see the eagles of light below and its shine was a little in the way, but then it moved on. Don't you remember, Ursa? We were watching together."

"Yes, I do vaguely remember seeing it."

"So it was there and then it moved on rather suddenly?" asked Harley. "Did you see anyone or anything nearby? I'm trying to work out who stole it."

Proxima shook his head. "No, I'm certain it was quite alone. I saw it heading eastwards." He pointed across the sky. "Isn't that right, Ursa?"

"Yes, I do believe it was all by itself."

"But why did it suddenly head east? What's there?" Harley took her small binoculars from her belt and looked out of the glass dome in that direction. In the distance she could vaguely make out dark pointed silhouettes, slightly lighter than the night sky. "The Copper Mountains," she breathed. "But why?" She looked back to the stars. "You have a better vantage point. Can you see the Moon behind the Copper Mountains?"

After gazing inquisitively eastwards, the stars shrugged. "I'm afraid not."

"Well, it can't have disappeared into thin air."

"Wait," said Vega, peering through tiny opera glasses. "There does appear to be a faint white glow by one of the mountains."

"You're right!" said Ursa, squinting. "It's coming from a cave. Most irregular."

Harley jumped back from the telescope. "Thank you! That's all been a great help."

"Are you going so soon? We haven't had a chance to sing you a number from the *Star Shimmer Cabaret*," said Vega.

"Next time, I promise!" Harley called, dashing back down the spiral steps. This was the biggest lead she had. The Moon was last seen heading over the Copper Mountains, and not only that, but her conversation with the stars had also given her more than she'd hoped for: a motive.

Grandpa Eden was waiting for Harley outside the star-chatter observatory with Cosmo.

"Cosmo came over to see if he could help

find Grandpa Elliot's watch and said you'd be here, so I thought we'd pick you up and give you a ride back in the tri-wheel trundle bike."

"Any luck with the watch?" she asked Cosmo.

"Not yet," he replied. "But I have an idea. How about you?"

"Yes, what is it, Harley? You're positively glowing," said Grandpa Eden.

"I have a lead on the missing Moon and I know what to do next," she declared. Although the theory she was developing didn't quite explain the other objects reported missing, she decided to tackle the Moon first and solve the other enigmas later.

Harley fixed Cosmo with a determined stare. "We have to go to the Copper Mountains." She went on to explain what the stars had seen the night of the circus.

"That's the best lead we've got. But … isn't that rather a long way? My mum isn't going to like it one bit."

Harley frowned. "She might if Grandpa Eden comes with us. Will you take us to the Copper Mountains in the trundle bike? Please, Grandpa?"

"You're quite sure it was last seen heading that way?"

"Absolutely."

"Then we must go." Grandpa Eden smiled. "If Cosmo gets permission from his mum, of course."

"What about school?" asked Cosmo. "Mum's definitely not going to like me missing it."

"How about if it was part of our school circus project? We could collect the liquid fire from the Copper Mountains along the way."

"Good idea! I'll speak to Mum and get packing."

"And we'd better speak to Grandpa Elliot and convince him too."

After they had dropped Cosmo back home and got settled in at Hitch House, they explained their plan to Grandpa Elliot.

"How long will it take you?"

"Usually it would take a day or two, but things aren't quite working like that at the moment," said Grandpa Eden.

"But what about school tomorrow? They can't miss that."

"If things carry on at this rate, Harley will have graduated from university within the year! No, I think Harley and Cosmo are on to something, and whatever has happened to knock the Moon out of the sky, we need to bring it back."

Grandpa Elliot nodded. "I'll speak to Professor Spark."

"We'd better take a tent. The trundle bike will get us so far, but the Copper Mountains are rugged, and we'll have to travel some of the way on foot."

"That's settled, then," said Harley with a grin. "We'll leave in the morning."

Sprocket barked.

"Yes, of course you're coming too!"

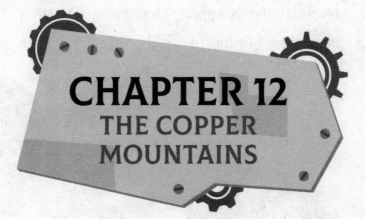

CHAPTER 12
THE COPPER MOUNTAINS

On the road out of Forgetown, Harley, Cosmo, and Grandpa Eden spotted some posters that had been put up at the side of the road. They read: "Give us back our moon", "Go away!" and "Thieves!" It seemed so unfair that people were blaming the circus, and it all made Harley more determined to resolve it as soon as possible.

They passed the circus, along the road

to the side of the Rusty River, and onwards towards the Copper Mountains. As they continued, beautiful fields brimming with yellow flowers came into view and they drove beside Tangerine Lake, which was one of her favourite spots to go camping.

Harley and her grandpas had camped in the Copper Mountain area for the summer ever since she could remember. Grandpa Eden loved the different wildlife, like the fields of trumpet flowers with their yellow fluted petals which whistled in the wind. They dripped with nectar and were favourites of the bronzlebees. Grandpa Elliot liked the peaceful atmosphere and having a break from the newspaper, and Harley loved to explore the different lakes and small forest glades with Sprocket.

After a short while they stopped for lunch, which turned into dinner on account of the shorter days, then they drove a bit further, passing small weaving brooks as the path twisted more and the land became rockier. Soon, evening descended and they had to stop to pitch their tent. Finding a mossy clearing, they got to work, with Grandpa Eden insisting they double peg the ropes on account of the strong gusts of wind which had been happening lately.

They soon had a fire lit and they cooked sausages over the flames, then popped corn in a pan, to Sprocket's delight.

"He loves to yip every time there's a pop," said Harley. "He might not eat it, but he certainly enjoys it!"

"You can't beat the great outdoors. It sure makes you feel close to nature." Grandpa Eden sucked in a long breath of air.

"I've never been camping," Cosmo declared suddenly.

"Really?" asked Harley, surprised.

"My parents aren't too keen. We do have holidays, usually to far-off, fancy places with hotels, but I'd really much rather do this."

The next morning they emerged from the tent to see the sun rise over the majestic, golden-brown zigzags of the Copper Mountains. They packed away the tent and carried on in the trundle bike until they were at the foot of the mountains.

"This is where we leave the bike. The road carries on east, but we need to go that way, where there are no roads."

They put on their backpacks and headed into the mountains.

"Wow, there are so many plants here I've never seen!" said Cosmo.

"This golden grass is unique to the area. It's tough as titanium and flexible too, so it makes excellent seat belts. You won't find it anywhere else in Inventia," said Grandpa Eden. "And this purple flower can usually only be seen in the height of summer. What with the seasons being upside down at the moment, they seem to be out early. I think I'll take a cutting back for the greenhouse, as it does make a supremely effective dye."

"Fascinating," said Cosmo, bending down to examine one.

Cosmo was the only person Harley knew who loved plants as much as Grandpa Eden. As for herself, she just loved being outdoors and on an adventure. She felt bad that Grandpa Elliot wasn't there, but he had to keep working on the latest updates for the *Forgetown Daily*.

Before long, the sun set once more, and they set up the tent for another quick sleep. Grandpa Eden had brought along some self-heating soup cans, and Sprocket used his internal heater to bake rolls. Then before they knew it, it was light again and they were back hiking further into the mountains. Harley wore her sturdy old boots, which felt good on her feet. She'd missed wearing them while being uniform-perfect

Harley with uncomfortable T-bar shoes.

"How do we know we're going in the right direction?" asked Cosmo.

"The stars saw a glowing light coming from a cave. The largest caves are in this area, so as soon as the sun sets again, we'll see if we can see the glow." They stopped on a rocky crag where they had a good view, then waited for the sun to set while they ate blueberry muffins and drank hot chocolate, courtesy of Sprocket's hidden compartments.

It wasn't too long before the blue sky turned to pink and peach, then darkened to a duskier blue.

"Over there!" said Harley.

A glow shone from a cave a short distance below.

"Lead the way with your lights, Sprocket,"

said Grandpa Eden. "Watch your step, everyone."

Carefully they made their way towards the cave. Outside, Harley told the others that she would go in first.

Tentatively, she stepped inside. At the far end of the cave, looking forlorn and sitting by a fire, was the Moon! It was big enough to fill her bedroom. She couldn't believe it was here, the thing that had been in the sky ever since she could remember, shining bright and tipping the Iron Forest with milky light. Although now it was looking decidedly grey.

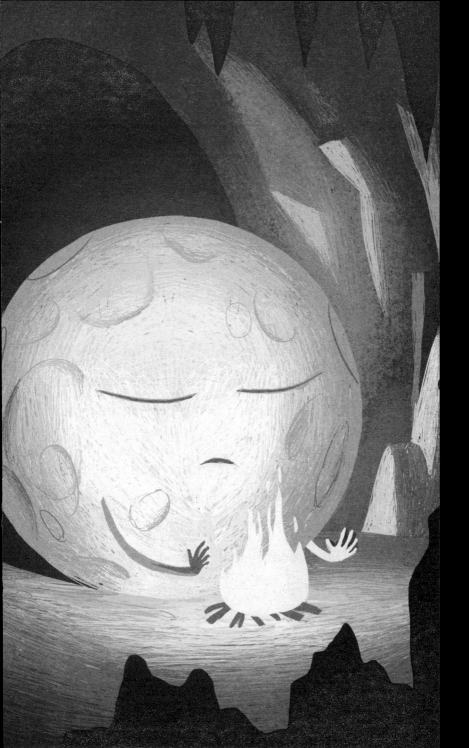

"Er, hello," Harley called.

She looked around, and a worrying thought suddenly struck her: what if her theory was wrong and perhaps thieves had kidnapped the Moon for a ransom?

The Moon stared at her in shock for a moment, then said in a low, miserable voice, "Go away."

"Excuse me, sir, Mr Moon, my name is Harley Hitch, and we've come a very long way to find you. Are you being held against your will?"

The Moon gave a dry, depressed non-laugh. "Who would even be bothered enough about me to do that?"

"Did someone steal you and put you here?" she persisted.

"Nobody cares about me." The Moon let

out a sigh heavy enough to sink ships. "I bet no one's even noticed I'm not around."

Harley frowned. What she suspected was true: the Moon was feeling dreadfully neglected and alone.

"You might feel that way, but it's really not true." She had to do her best to reassure him and lift him out of his gloom.

"Life won't be any different without me. I mean, no one even bothers to call me by my real name, they just call me the Moon. There are thousands of moons, millions out there in the Universe, yet no one cares enough to even consider I'm an individual." He turned away from Harley.

"You're so wrong!" she blurted, although he had a good point about his name. She'd always thought of him simply as "the Moon".

"Really? Who would even give me a second look when you've got the twinkling dazzle of the stars in the night sky?"

"Lots of people – and other creatures, for that matter!"

"And I'm ugly." The Moon let out another mournful sigh and floated further into the cave.

Harley beckoned for Grandpa Eden and Cosmo to join her, then followed the Moon.

"Ugly? No! Why would you think that?"

"Have you seen my craters during the first quarter? I'm nothing compared to the stars. I'm just a rocky lump of boring nothingness. Even my light isn't my own. It's all borrowed from the Sun: I just reflect its light."

Harley made her voice extra jaunty to try and lift the Moon's monotone sadness. "Well, I think your craters are beautiful. All of you is."

"You're just saying that."

"Because I mean it. Go back to the sky. Back to where you belong."

The Moon shook its head sadly. "My mind is made up. I'm staying here, for ever. Nobody cares, so neither do I."

"You're wrong. Maybe you're feeling overlooked, but it's not the case."

"Thank you, strange little human, but you should go now. There's nothing you can say that will change my mind." He shrank back against the wall and slunk into a sad heap.

The firelight glow flickered off the walls and the Moon's cratered surface.

Grandpa Eden and Cosmo shrugged. What more could they do?

But Harley never gave up on things easily. She frowned and concentrated her thoughts.

There must be some way to entice the Moon back outside and make him see he was wrong about himself.

An idea blossomed in Harley's imagination. "All right, Mr Moon. I understand how you feel, and that there is nothing I can say to convince you. But would you perhaps do something for me?"

"Why would I do something for you? I barely know you. I barely know anyone, or have any friends. I was a lone Moon in a sorrowful sky, now I'm a lone Moon in a sorrowful cave. Leave me alone."

Harley knelt before the Moon and gave a friendly smile.

"Don't be like that. All I'm asking is for you to take one last trip to the sky, let's say around five days from now. I'll send you a sign when the time is right. And if you're not convinced after that, then you can come back here and live your life in peace and I'll never bother you again."

"You'll never bother me again?"

"Never."

The Moon sighed mournfully. "I can't promise anything."

"Just try." Harley smiled. "It'll be worth it."

And they left the cave.

"What was that about?" asked Cosmo.

"I have a plan. But it's not going to be easy to pull off."

Grandpa Eden smiled and shook his head. "At this rate you're having more plans than breakfasts!"

"What's the plan?" Cosmo asked.

She beamed. "Something big."

CHAPTER 13

THE BIG PLAN

They started back across the Copper Mountains, but they hadn't gone far before they needed to pitch the tent again.

The short days were frustrating, as Harley needed to get going with her idea.

"Are you ready to tell us yet?" asked Cosmo.

"Not quite. I need to get back to Forgetown and pay a visit to the star-chatter observatory first."

"Just as long as you know what you're doing." Grandpa Eden smiled. "I'm just going to gather a little more wood for the fire and collect some liquid fire while we're here. Professor Spark mentioned she was running low on school stocks and I noticed a few vents not far away. Sprocket, will you light the way for me?"

"We can help," said Harley.

"No, you stay warm by the fire. We won't be long."

"Come on, at least tell me something about your plan," Cosmo persisted.

"All right. It's to do with making the Moon see how brilliant he really is, just as he is."

Cosmo laughed.

"What's so funny about that?"

"It's just…"

"Spit it out."

"It's you."

"Me?"

"This term, I've felt like I've lost you."

"What do you mean?"

"You've been doing your very best to conform to what you think you should be like, just to get Pupil of the Term. And I think you're missing a little of what makes you special."

"What do you mean?" It felt like a punch to the guts, but as she thought about it, she knew exactly what he meant. There she was, telling the Moon how special he was when she'd been doing her very best to go against all her own instincts that made her unique. "I know I've been a bit different, but…"

"I've popped over several times to help

Grandpa Eden in the garden because you told him you didn't want to get messy, and I know he misses your help. You're usually so chatty and friendly to the robots at school, but now you barely even look their way. You've hardly had time to play with Sprocket either."

"I've been trying not to get into trouble!"

"I know. But is it really worth it, for this badge?"

"I've wanted it for so long."

"All I'm saying is that you're usually like..." He thought for a moment. "Rainbows."

"Rainbows?" Harley wasn't entirely sure what he meant, but she thought it was probably the nicest thing anyone had ever said to her.

"Let's just say, these past few days, since the circus, it's been good to have old Harley back."

They sat in companionable silence and soon

Grandpa Eden and Sprocket returned with some more firewood.

"Grandpa, I'm sorry I haven't been helping much with the garden lately."

He squeezed her shoulder. "There's nothing to apologize for."

Harley made a decision, an extension to her plan to save the Moon. Although it meant throwing away what she'd worked for with her be-perfect Harley plan, she had to stop trying to be something she wasn't. It wasn't worth being Pupil of the Term if she had to give up being herself.

"You look like you've had another revelation." Grandpa Eden passed her a marshmallow on a stick to toast in the fire.

"I think I have." She glanced at Cosmo with his floppy fringe and too-big glasses and thought how her friend was just as he should be. She couldn't be Professor Fretshaw's idea of "perfect"; she had to be her own. "I'll focus on my plan, and you carry on looking for the other missing objects. We know that the Moon was responsible for its own disappearance, but that doesn't account for the other missing things. We have to find the real reason and help the Monocle sisters."

"I'm still stumped," said Cosmo. "Usually, I'd suggest a trip to the library, but I'm not sure it'll help with this… How about a trip to the Rusty River after school tomorrow?"

"Excellent idea. You're finally coming around to my way of thinking, Always trust the fish." Harley smiled.

The next day, they picked up a fishing rod from home and hurried to Rusty River.

Cosmo cast the line. "What if I don't get a bite?"

"Cosmo, are you being a worry pants again? Have faith in the ri—"

The line tugged.

"Quick, reel it in!"

A bronze, flat fish leaped into Cosmo's hands, and after an appropriately dramatic pause declared, "Do not listen to what they say. Go and see." Then it wriggled out of his fingers and splashed back into the water.

"Sorry, but that makes no sense at all," said Harley.

Cosmo shuffled his feet in thought for a minute, then said, "No, it does make sense! Everybody is saying the objects have been stolen and are blaming the circus, right?"

"Yes."

"But that doesn't mean they've been stolen. The fish is telling me to go and see for myself. They may all simply be lost and have a rational explanation. I need to retrace each object to the moment it went missing, which might not be when everyone thinks."

"Oh-kay… Where are you going to start?"

"Your Grandpa Elliot's pocket watch. It went missing the night of the circus, but when exactly?"

She thought back to that night. It had been dark. "It was pitch black when we were walking back because that's when the Moon disappeared, even though we didn't realize it at the time. Grandpa Elliot tripped."

"He might have lost it when he fell!"

They hurried back to the place where Grandpa Elliot had fallen and began searching along the edge of the road. Sprocket yelped and sprang towards Harley with Grandpa Elliot's pocket watch in his mouth.

"Excellent work, wonder pup!" Harley stroked him enthusiastically behind the ears.

The sky darkened again. "Right, you take

the list and continue to find an explanation for all the lost objects. Trace back where they were last seen and don't stop until you find them. Speak to Grandpa Elliot about publishing a story in tomorrow's morning paper so that everyone in Forgetown knows there is a perfectly rational explanation behind all the disappearances."

Cosmo nodded. "What are you going to do?"

"I'm going to visit the star-chatter observatory, and I need to speak to the circus, and a few of the professors, and some friends."

"Your plan sounds ambitious."

"It is! Oh, and there is one other little thing you can do for me."

After telling Cosmo her request, Harley carried on with her plan. There was a whole lot of explaining and persuading to do, but she managed to achieve what she'd hoped for.

Exhausted, she finally made it back to Hitch House. Grandpa Elliot gave her a big hug. "I hear you've been extremely busy."

"Grandpa Elliot, could you print this as a fancy poster for me at the newspaper in the morning?"

He looked at the piece of paper and smiled. "I certainly can."

CHAPTER 14
THE MOON EXTRAVAGANZA

Preparations for the plan carried on throughout the next day, with everyone involved working tirelessly to do their bit. Grandpa Elliot brought back the poster. It was decorated with red and gold, and it stated:

MONOCLES'
MARVELLOUS
MACHINES

BRING YOU A
ONCE-IN-A-LIFETIME,
FOR-ONE-NIGHT-ONLY
PERFORMANCE:

THE MOON
EXTRAVAGANZA!
STARTS 7 P.M. SHARP

"It's perfect, thank you!" She sent the poster with one of Miss Li's mechanical postal pigeons, giving it detailed instructions for locating the Copper Mountain cave, then dashed off to her room to send some late transmissions telling everybody to meet up for rehearsals in the morning.

Rehearsals at the circus site went surprisingly well. They managed to set the stage up in the open air with all the mechanics needed, and then ran through the whole show – except for the part featuring the stars, who couldn't appear in daylight, but who had assured Harley they were rehearsing their part with commitment.

There was time for a quick break before getting ready for the show, so Sprocket poured Harley a quick cocoa and ejected a blueberry muffin from his side.

"How have you got on with the other lost objects?" Harley asked Cosmo.

"All accounted for. When time got rushed, everyone got rushed, so of course many things got overlooked or forgotten. And false rumours about the Monocle sisters didn't help matters." He took his list from his pocket. "Watch found in the bushes, trowel tidied away in Daisy's drawer, sock found under the bed, Professor Fretshaw's glasses were still with Primbot, she'd forgotten to pick them up, and the very best one was Fenelda's necklace."

"Where did you find it?"

"I didn't. It turns out her every-help-bot found it under her pillow when she was cleaning several days ago. Fenelda kept the news to herself because she was too embarrassed after anonymously sending an article to the newspaper, listing the missing objects, calling it suspicious and insinuating that there were thieves at the circus."

"Ah, typical Fenelda. No wonder she didn't resist when I asked her to play a part in the show. She was obviously feeling guilty."

"And the brilliant thing is that your Grandpa Elliot is going to print a story in the newspaper clearing the circus name and showing that there was a rational explanation for each object and that people overreacted because of time speeding up."

"That's great."

"How are things going for you?"

"I think we're all set for the show. Although there is one more thing I need to do first."

"Can I help?" asked Cosmo.

Harley shook her head. "Thanks, but not with this. I'll meet you back here before seven, then we've just got to hope that the Moon shows up."

Back at Hitch House, Harley rushed to the greenhouse to find Grandpa Eden. "Have you still got the blueberry bushes, woad and indigo plants?"

"I thought you'd never ask." He winked. "They're all mixed up and ready to go!"

The room suddenly grew dim as a large

object blocked the sunlight streaming in through the window.

"Hey, what's that outside?"

"It appears to be the Monocle sisters' giant robot!"

Harley hurried to the door. The robot was carrying a brown paper package tied with a red-and-gold bow.

"The Monocle sisters said they have made this for you," the robot said in its flat mechanical tone.

"Thank you!" said Harley taking the package. "I wonder what it is…"

Backstage, Harley drummed her fingers nervously against a tent pole.

"You look spectacular," said Cosmo. Her hair was now blue, and she was wearing a short red jacket that the Monocle sisters had created especially for her with long tails, brass buttons, and golden shoulder tassels. She had matching trousers and long, polished boots.

"Thank you, so do you! Your cog bow tie is my favourite." She took a breath. "What if the Moon doesn't come?"

"He will. Who could resist such an invitation?"

Seven o'clock struck.

The drum roll began.

Harley put her hands on her hips for a moment. She could do this. Then she burst through the curtains and into the spotlight. There was an air of silent anticipation in the big top tent – which now had its top removed. She looked up to the sky, crossed her fingers and squeezed. "Please, Moon," she whispered. Her palms began to sweat as she wondered if it had all been for nothing and would turn out to be yet another huge thing-gone-wrong in her history of mishaps.

Then a thin, glowing slither of white appeared on the horizon.

"The Moon!" Harley dashed forwards on

the stage and spread her arms wide to the sky, shouting, "Let the *Great Moon Extravaganza* begin!" She took her shiny black top hat in one hand and bowed.

Above, the stars had broken with tradition and come down to earth especially to watch the show close up. They applauded wildly from the sky a short distance away to the front of the stage, along with Cosmo, her grandpas, all the members of Monocles' Marvellous Machines, and the professors and classmates waiting in the wings.

The eagle drones took flight and zoomed into formation, spelling:

WELCOME, MOON!

The Moon ambled sheepishly across the sky, then settled before them. "What's all this about then?" he asked in his monotone sad voice.

"We're putting on a show, and you are our only audience. So I'm pretty glad you showed up." She winked, then gestured to the sky. "First, may I introduce to you a celestial performance by the stars of an original opera, written especially for you, titled—" She looked at her prompt card. "—*You Make Our Nights Bright!*"

Ursa Major took the centre of the sky a short distance above the stage. Sparkles radiated off her shimmering moon-bright gown and she burst into song. In the opera, Ursa played the Moon and Proxima and Vega didn't notice her until she sang her sweetest song, and they joined her and sang in beautiful harmony together.

When they finished, they took theatrical bows. Harley looked to the Moon. Was it working? The Moon stared at the stage. It was impossible to read his expression. Then the hint of a smile spread across his face and he began to clap. Everyone joined in and soon the Moon was applauding vigorously.

Ringmaster Harley took the stage once more. "Next, we have the moths of Inventia showing their appreciation." Harley had called on Professor Thorax, whose specialism was entomology, or bugology as the students liked to call it, to communicate with the moths. "Well, I'm not entirely sure how they are going to do it, but I guess we'll see!" Then thousands of moths filled the sky, their delicate foil wings glittering in the sky like sunlight on waves. They flocked around the Moon, circling him, and he laughed at the tickle of their wings. Then the eagle drones lit the sky with their lights and the moths followed their glow as they flew into the air above the stage and formed the shape of a heart together.

The Moon clutched his chest. "Simply beautiful," he said.

Everyone clapped.

"Thank you to the moths of Inventia, who I think are very pleased to see you! And now, for our next performance, I give you Cosmo

Willoughby and his poem of the seasons, titled '23.5 Degrees'."

Cosmo took to the stage. Harley noticed his hands shaking a little and he shuffled his feet uncomfortably. "You can do it, Cosmo," she whispered.

He took a breath.

"Winter, Spring, Summer, Autumn,
The flow of nature
The cycle of balance
Where would we be without our seasons?
Lost for ever in summer, or winter?
No February snowdrops,
Spring daffo-nils,

Summer brings only frozen roses,
Silvercorns don't drop in autumn

Without you, our seasons would disappear
Or become extreme.
You keep our tilt stable
Our wobble in check.
It is you who brings our balanced bouquet."

With a sideways glance to Harley, he mouthed, "Was that all right?"

Harley beamed and gave him a big thumbs up.

The Moon clapped. "I didn't even realize I kept the planet at a tilt, or that the seasons needed me. I'm so touched," he said, his voice sounding more buoyant.

Harley resumed her place centre stage. "And now for our next performance, something I'm especially excited for…"

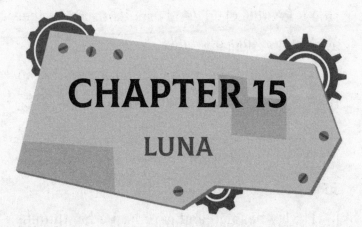

CHAPTER 15

LUNA

"Sprocket, the grandpas and friends bring you …
the Tidal Dance!" Harley left the stage and
Grandpa Eden and Grandpa Elliot stepped into
place on opposite sides, holding great swathes
of blue fabric.

In the wings, Sprocket was dressed in a
crab outfit, the garden-bots of Cogworks were
dressed as snails, Letti and Asma were sea

anemones, Rufus was a limpet, and Fenelda stood red-cheeked and shuffling her feet awkwardly in a large starfish costume.

The band started and the grandpas began their dance on the stage, rippling and waving the material so that it looked like the rise and fall of waves.

"I've never looked so ridiculous in all my life," said Fenelda, turning to Harley with tight lips. "I can't believe you roped me into this."

"Well, Nel, you always want to be the star of everything, now's your chance. Go out there and embrace your inner starfish." Harley shoved her on to the stage, with a little smile to herself.

While the grandpas danced the ebb and flow of the tides, Sprocket pranced happily around them in his crab outfit along with the other sea creatures, who all danced happily

among the waves. Fenelda was a little stiff, but Harley thought she at least gave it a good effort.

Suddenly, the grandpas laid down their fabric and curled up on the floor, signifying the end of the tides. The music ceased and the crabs, mussels, starfish and snails all stopped dancing and gradually withered dramatically to the floor to lie utterly silent and still.

The Moon was leaning forward, watching intently and looking incredibly sad. A tear rolled down his cheek.

Harley gave a nod and the grandpas rose and began dancing and raising the material tides again, the sea creatures came back to life and the Moon cheered and clapped.

The performers bowed and left the stage

and Harley jogged back on in her ringmaster splendour. "How to follow such a powerful performance? You'll be pleased to know that we can, because next in our line-up for the *Moon Extravaganza*, we have the Monocle trapeze artists with their interpretation of days."

The trapeze troupe were dressed as arrows, signifying the hands of time. Laser clocks projected into the sky and a large, self-playing drum beat a regular rhythm to the beat of seconds. The hoops and lines descended from the rigging above, and the troupe jumped up and started a slow movement around the clocks, swinging in time with the rhythm of the drum. The beat grew faster and the performers picked up their pace. Yet again the drum quickened, and soon the troupe was a dramatic blur flying through the sky, missing each other by a whisker. The Moon gasped. Then the drum gradually slowed and the performers gradually resumed a comforting regular pace to the beat of seconds.

When they had finished, they jumped back to the stage and bowed.

The Moon wiped his brow, then clapped. "That was very dramatic!"

"You see, even the hours in our days are linked to you," said Harley. "You're very attractive, and the Earth slows down its spinning because of you!" The Moon smiled and blushed. "And for our final performance this evening, with an original composition titled 'We'll Never be Over the Moon', I give you the newly formed Moon Orchestra!"

Professor Spark, Dr Orbit and Professor Horatio took to the stage. Each played their solo instrument: Professor Spark on the cello, Dr Orbit on the violin, and Professor Horatio on the viola. The instrumental piece flowed so that they all had their moment to show their individual and unique sound, before they reached a crescendo in a final cacophony of musical bliss, when all the self-playing instruments joined in.

The Moon cheered and cheered. "Bravo, bravo, all of you!"

For the grand finale, all the performers gathered on stage and the giant robot lifted Harley high into the air. It was higher than she expected, and her stomach flew to her chest.

After a long breath, she spread her arms and projected her voice as best she could. "You see, dear Moon, we are all proud of who you are, but we think you should be proud of who you are too. Crabs, mussels, starfish, snails – all of them rely on the tides for survival. Without life on our coasts, this would have effects for animals everywhere and could lead to extinctions. Without you, our days are short, and there would be a thousand days in a year! You help bring us a stable climate, and without you we would never experience the beauty of an eclipse.

"You make our lives shine bright, and your beauty is always changing in the night. We're sorry you felt overlooked, but we hope tonight's performance has shown you that we appreciate you, because you are perfect, and we love you just the way you are. You are our one and only Moon."

Harley took off her top hat and took a bow.

She looked up. Everything had fallen utterly silent. Had it all been enough?

Then the Moon erupted with applause and smiled a smile that would brighten the gloomiest night. The grandpas joined in, Cosmo and the children from their class whooped, the Professors cheered, the members of Monocles' Marvellous Machines clapped and the biggest grin spread on Harley's face. They'd done it.

Everybody mingled and stayed to chat for a while at the end. The Moon floated over to Harley, who was standing with Grandpa Elliot. "Thank you for what you did this evening."

"It was a team effort." She smiled. "I hope you now know that without you, things in Inventia would have evolved very differently. And there's not a person, creature or celestial being in this world that doesn't have flaws, but I think the flaws can be beautiful too."

"I'd better get back to the sky. There's work to be done."

"Before you go, there is one last thing..."

"Yes?"

Grandpa Elliot passed him a scroll of paper tied with a silver ribbon. The Moon unfurled it.

"What is it?"

"It's your name certificate. Grandpa Elliot

organized it for you through his city contacts."

"My proper name?"

With a nod, Harley said, "It's Luna, isn't it? I think it's the most beautiful name I've ever heard."

A smile broke out on his face.

"Of course you could be Luna Moon, if you want to be!"

Luna laughed. "Harley, I don't know how to thank you for this evening. I feel as though everything is as it should be."

"You don't need to thank me. In fact, it's done me good too." It had been strange, but she hadn't felt more herself since last term.

With that, Luna gave a huge grin and launched himself back to the sky, high above them. "Thank you! Don't be a stranger!" he called. As he rose higher, he began to shine once more.

Harley waved and smiled to herself, a content warmth filling her chest.

She went over to thank the Monocle sisters for helping her and letting them use their site for the performance.

"It was our pleasure," said one of the sisters. Harley still couldn't be sure which was Maria and which was Marissa, although now she was getting to know them she thought perhaps Maria was just a little taller.

"And if you ever want a job as a presenter, we'd be happy to have you join us, Harley," said the other.

Their words made her glow inside. "Thank you! Maybe one day I'll take you up on that."

CHAPTER 16
A NEW TRADITION

The end of term came around swiftly. Mostly, things returned to normal: the tides returned, the days became longer again, the moths went back to their routines, and Professor Fretshaw was back to looking at Harley suspiciously, as though Harley might get up to mischief at any moment.

Monocles' Marvellous Machines resumed

their tour of Inventia and Professor Spark forwarded their project designs for new acts. Harley and Cosmo's flame-juggling robots won second place, and the winner was Letti and Asma's rainbow canon, which shot rainbows out on demand. The Monocle sisters said it was just the sort of positivity that Inventia needed and they loved the idea of leaving rainbows wherever they went.

A new tradition took hold in the Hitch family; they called it the Luna picnic. On nights when Luna was in full view, Harley, the grandpas and Sprocket would take a midnight picnic to a clearing in the Iron Forest where they all would sit and catch up with everything Luna had seen that month. Cosmo would join them too because, as Harley said, he was practically one of the family now anyway.

Tonight, they sat on their tartan picnic blanket in an open area surrounded by golden hazel trees.

"So you didn't win Pupil of the Term?" asked Luna.

Harley took a sip of cocoa and shook her head. Her grades had been good, but Fenelda's had been slightly better because Harley had missed a bit of work when she'd gone to the Copper Mountains.

As it turned out, Letti's grades had been just as good overall as Fenelda's, and her win in the circus invention project secured her Pupil of the Term, much to Fenelda's annoyance. Harley was pleased for Letti because she was a good friend and always kind. Harley liked it when quiet people were noticed too.

"Well, that's too bad you didn't win," said Luna. "I should have liked to have seen that shiny gold light bulb pinned to you." Then he winked theatrically at Grandpa Eden.

"What's all that winking about?" asked Harley suspiciously.

"I don't know what you mean," said Luna, winking again.

Grandpa Eden nodded. "Sprocket, I think it's time."

A flap opened in Sprocket's top panel

where he sometimes stored a muffin snack. Instead, there was a small silver Moon badge. It glimmered and glistened with moonlight.

"We had it made in Inventia to Luna's specifications," said Grandpa Elliot. He pinned the badge on Harley's dungarees.

Looking down at the shiny pin, Harley couldn't have felt prouder.

Luna smiled. "You may not have won Pupil of the Term, but you will forever be an Honorary Moonbeam."

"Honorary Moonbeam?" Harley breathed. It sounded magical.

"It's a new thing," said Luna. "For people who embrace individuality – and help others do the same."

"Wow, I don't know what to say!" Harley's heart swelled with warmth. She knew that Professor Fretshaw valued an idea of perfection. It was one way of viewing things, but it wasn't necessarily right. Being true to who she was and thinking outside the box was what Harley did best. Sometimes it went to plan, and sometimes it went rather wrong, but as her grandpas often said, sometimes you have to get things wrong to learn how to get them right.

"Perhaps that fish at Rusty River was on to something," said Cosmo. "Nothing is so certain as the unexpected."

"Never mock the fish. The fish are always right." Harley laughed. She looked down at her Moonbeam badge. "Can I keep this for ever?"

"Absolutely," said Luna.

They chatted, laughed and drank hot chocolate long into the night.

As for Pupil of the Term? Although Harley realized it was a less important to her than before...

There was always next time.

ACKNOWLEDGEMENTS

Continued thanks for all of those who support my books, both within publishing and the many educators, librarians, booksellers, bloggers and general reading enthusiasts.

Thank you to the team at Scholastic UK in all departments who have played a part in this book and my eternal thanks to Linas Alsenas, Kate Shaw, George Ermos, Jamie Gregory, Harriet Dunlea, Pete Matthews, and Sarah Dutton.

A special hello to all the young coglings

out there. I hope you can, like Harley, be who you want to be in life. Always dream BIG and remember, you never fail if you are willing to try.

Vashti Hardy grew up in West Sussex between the hills and the sea, scrambling through brambles and over pebbles. Her middle-grade fantasy novels are now published across the world in several languages. Her debut, *Brightstorm*, was shortlisted for the Waterstones Children's Book Prize and Books Are My Bag Readers Awards, and her second book, *Wildspark*, won the Blue Peter Book Award 'Best Story' in 2020. Vashti now lives in both West Sussex and Lancashire with her husband and three children.

Vashtihardy.com
Twitter @vashti_hardy
Instagram vashtihardyauthor

... n illustrator, maker and ... gland. He works digitally ... g all things curious and ... ways trying to incorporate ... e various world cultures he ... res.

@georgermos

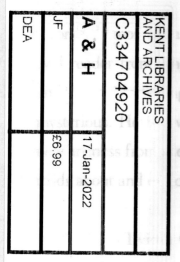

DON'T MISS HARLEY'S OTHER ADVENTURE

HARLEY HITCH AND THE IRON FOREST

VASHTI HARDY

ILLUSTRATED BY GEORGE ERMOS